'Kiss her! Y... mistletoe.'

Ben and Thomase... plastic flower hung .... before they stared at each other in total surprise.

Everyone in the pub was eager for them to kiss, and Thomasena felt as though she'd just entered another dimension. What was going on here? Her skin started to tingle with anticipation and fear. He wouldn't kiss her...would he?

'Ready to get this over and done with?'

'What? You're going to—?'

'Relax, Tom. Trust me.' He winked at her and took both of her hands in his. Breathing out slowly, he raised them to his lips and pressed a light kiss to each one, before rubbing his thumb tenderly over the spot in a gentle caress.

The action was enough to take her breath away, and her eyes reflected her pleasure in the romantic and gallant gesture. Her knees began to weaken, and when he glanced at her she knew her eyes reflected not only surprise but something more...something strange and powerful...and it was something she'd never felt before. An awareness of just how strong, how close and how male Ben really was.

'Welcome to Blaytent Springs, Thomasena,' he murmured.

Lucy Clark is a husband and wife team. They live in South Australia with their two children. Between them, they have tutored and lectured in the craft of romance-writing, and hold degrees in Computing Science and Economics. They both find inspiration in their daily walks, are mad movie buffs, and delight in spending time with their children holidaying at various locations around Australia.

Recent titles by the same author:

HIS CHRISTMAS PROPOSAL

BY
LUCY CLARK

MILLS & BOON
Pure reading pleasure

First published in Great Britain 2007
Harlequin Mills & Boon Limited,
Eton House, 18-24 Paradise Road, Richmond, Surrey TW9 1SR

© Anne Clark and Peter Clark 2007

ISBN: 978 0 263 85275 2

Set in Times Roman 10½ on 12¼ pt
03-1107-49329

Printed and bound in Spain
by Litografia Rosés, S.A., Barcelona

HIS CHRISTMAS PROPOSAL

For Kath & Belinda,
who are an incredible support and who understand the
persistence and dedication needed to do the work.
2 Peter-3:18

CHAPTER ONE

'BEN! Ben? Where are you?' Linda walked through the consulting rooms, calling for him. 'Ben?'

'I'm here,' he called back from the supply storeroom.

'What are you doing? You're going to be late.'

'Keep your shirt on, Lin.'

'You should talk.' She held out a short-sleeved cotton shirt. 'Put this on and button it up. You don't want to scare the new doctor away.'

Ben finished putting the last of the stock up on the top shelf. 'The plane doesn't arrive for another five minutes and the airstrip isn't exactly far away.' He raised his eyebrows.

'Nowhere in this town is far away and the plane has already landed.'

'What?'

'Didn't you hear it?'

'No.' He thought that odd as he came out of the small supply storeroom, which could fit two people in it at a squeeze. His mind was pretty attuned to the drone of the plane engines, especially when they were bringing relief in the way of food, clothing and the necessary medical supplies he regularly ordered off the Internet. Ben walked to his consulting room and pulled on his bush hat. 'When did it arrive?'

'Two minutes ago.' Lin shook the shirt at him again. 'Put this on,' she instructed. 'You'll scare the new doctor if the first thing she sees of you is sweaty, naked flesh.'

'Oh, I don't know.' Ben waggled his eyebrows up and down in a suggestive manner. 'Perhaps it will entice her to stay for ever.'

Lin laughed without humour. 'Ha. Like that's gonna happen. Who wants to live out here in the middle of nowhere?'

He shrugged. 'Us.' Ben slipped on his sunglasses and snatched up the shirt hanging from Lin's finger. 'Back soon. Everything is ready for the new doctor? Right?'

'Yes. Everything except the welcoming committee. Just go.'

Ben chuckled over Linda's exasperation as he walked out the door and down the wide footpath, swatting flies as he went. He hoped this new doctor was going to work out, unlike the last few he'd managed to lure out here. He grinned as he glanced around the one-road town of Blaytent Springs. It had all the comforts of home, as far as he was concerned. General store, which also acted as the petrol station, a vet, a doctor's surgery, tennis court, a couple of houses and a pub. Let the Lord bless the outback Aussie pub, which was also the hotel for any travellers passing through.

'How are you going to like this, big city doctor?' he mused, chuckling as he walked across the road, stepping off the large, wide gutters that had already dried from the afternoon rains. Swatting the flies away with the shirt he still held in his hand, Ben headed up the dirt road that led to the airstrip. 'G'day, Bertie,' he called as he walked into the tin shed that was Blaytent Spring's airport terminal.

'Hey. There ya are, Doc.' Bertie pointed to the woman

standing in the corner of the building, a boy almost the same height as her standing behind—both with a look of complete shock and a hint of disdain on their faces. 'Gotta delivery for ya.' Bertie grinned, his white teeth shining out against his black skin.

'Thanks, mate.' Ben headed over, taking off his sunglasses and hat. 'G'day.' He held out a hand. 'I'm Ben Caruthers. You must be Dr Bates, yeah?'

Thomasena Bates tried not to shrink back from the sight of this almost naked stranger who was offering his hand. She had watched him casually stroll into the place, her gaze travelling over him, taking in his long tanned legs, khaki shorts, socks and workboots. The sight of his tanned torso, which held a smattering of light-coloured chest hair, was enough to make her hyperventilate—not only from wondering whether she'd made the right decision to come to the outback of Australia but also because it had been quite a while since she'd seen such an incredible specimen of maleness.

'Mum,' James, her son, said between his teeth, and it was then Thomasena realised her new colleague was still holding out his hand. Mortification flooded through her as she realised she'd been gawking openly at the man but outwardly she squared her shoulders and raised her chin, giving the stranger a polite smile as she extended her hand.

He gripped it firmly in his and shook it heartily. 'Good strong handshake you've got there, Dr Bates.' Ben smiled at her and she felt her legs begin to weaken at the effect. She jerked her hand back as though burnt before forcing herself to calm down once more. She'd been a debutante and attended a Swiss finishing school. She was the epitome of decorum and elegance and had been in many situations when she'd been rankled by other people. Why, then, should Benjamin Caruthers, with his dark brown hair and rich, deep, chocolaty brown eyes be creating so much havoc within her? His presence was…consuming, and she wished he'd put his shirt on immediately—but the fact remained, he was merely her colleague for the next six months and *nothing more*. She could do this. She could live in the outback, work in the outback. What she thought of Dr Caruthers was irrelevant. She had her own agenda and starting a new life with her son was top of the list.

Thomasena looked him in the eyes as she spoke. 'Thank you, Dr Caruthers. And, please, call me Thomasena. This is my son, James.'

Ben tried not to raise his eyebrows at her smooth, well-modulated tones. He guessed they matched her designer clothes and whilst she was dressed in flat shoes, cool linen trousers and a cotton shirt—her ensemble probably costing more than the shed they were standing in—it also made him wish he'd donned the shirt, hoping her first impression of him didn't include the word *neanderthal* in it.

The boy shifted and Ben saw he was the same height as his mother. 'Jimmy. G'day, mate.' Ben shook hands with the young man. 'Welcome to the outback.' He hadn't missed the way Thomasena—was that really her name?—had seemed to bristle at the nickname for her son. Well, she'd have to get used to it, he decided. Out here, *everyone* had a nickname. It was a sign of outback affection.

'Thank you.' The boy's smile was as polite as his mother's.

'How old are you? Twelve? Thirteen?'

'Almost thirteen, sir.'

'Aah, you can drop the *sir* out here.' Ben chuckled. 'We're very informal—the lot of us. Ain't that right, Bertie?'

'Ya got that straight, Doc.' Bertie nodded to them.

'Right. Guess we'd better get your bags over to your

new home, eh? You two got hats?' As he spoke, he put his own hat and sunglasses back on and, thankfully, his cotton shirt. He quickly did up two of the buttons and she noticed he didn't seem to care or notice that he'd done it crookedly.

'Yes. Yes, we do,' Thomasena said, and picked up new bush hats from the pile of designer luggage she stood in front of, handing one to her son. 'I've done my outback research, Dr Caruthers.'

'It's Ben, and I'm pleased to hear it. OK.' He pointed to the suitcases. 'I'm hoping they have wheels—if not, we'll have to make a few trips.'

'Uh…why, yes, they do. Won't they all fit in your car?'

'I didn't bring my car. It's not that far. Down the road, turn right, about half a kilometre down the road and we're there.'

Thomasena gulped then remembered her manners and nodded.

Ben chuckled as he took two bags, leaving Thomasena with two backpacks, one handbag and three more suitcases. 'You may need to give us a hand, Bert.' He broke off as the sound of footsteps came closer, followed by laboured breathing. A moment later, a young girl came into the shed.

'Sorry, Dad. Sorry. I was going to be here but the plane was early and I was out at the springs, and, hi, there,' she finished, waving to the newcomers.

'This is my daughter, Matilda. Matty, for short.'

Thomasena's eyebrows rose. He had a daughter? Her opinion of him as a laid-back slob changed a little to one of intrigue. She glanced down at his left hand but it was ringless—as was hers. Was he married? Was he, like her, a single parent? The girl was tall and lanky but starting to get feminine curves. She was wearing swimming shorts and top, obligatory hat on her head and running shoes with no socks. A strip of white was across her nose and around her lips—zinc cream, although it was a little smeared. When she took the hat from her head, Thomasena was surprised her short blond hair was damp whilst the rest of her was quite dry.

They returned the greeting, then Ben said, 'Grab a bag, Mat. See you in the clinic, Bertie,' he said pointedly to the man.

'Nah, Doc. I ain't comin' in.'

'Then, I'll find you. You need that check-up, mate, and I ain't takin' no for an answer.'

'I don't need it, Doc,' Bertie continued to protest.

Ben put the bags down and looked at his friend thoughtfully. 'House call? Or we can do the check-up right now.'

Bertie looked around, as though trying to figure out his best escape route from the one-roomed shed. He gave Thomasena a wary look and Ben picked up on it.

'Or I could schedule an appointment here with the new lady doc. Perhaps you'd like her to treat you. She's certainly prettier to look at than my ugly mug.'

'Nah, Doc,' Bertie said again, but there was slight fear and uncertainty in his voice. 'Aah, no offence, missus. I'll see, uh…Doc Ben here, if ya don't mind.'

'Not at all,' Thomasena remarked, unsure of what was going on but determined to support her new colleague in any way she could. 'But if you don't happen to make the appointment, would you mind if I tagged along on the house call?'

'I'll be there,' Bertie promised quickly, and Thomasena nodded in satisfaction.

'All right, then.' She hefted a backpack onto her shoulders, added her shoulder-bag and picked up one of the suitcases, extending the handle. 'Shall we go?'

Ben stood stock-still for a moment, surprised at the way this classy city princess, for that was exactly what she looked like, had backed him up. Perhaps this was going to work out after all.

'Dad!' Matty said.

'Uh…yep. Let's go.'

Stepping out of the shade, the heat hit them like a small truck, accompanied by a group of flies. Thomasena was glad she had a hand free to swat the pesky insects away.

'You'll get used to it,' Ben said, shaking his head and blowing them away. 'So, Jimmy? Glad school's done for the year?'

'Yes, si— Uh, Ben.'

'Good, lad. Once school is done out here, Christmas fever sets in, but only once all the kids doing exams are finished. They let loose and go around to all the buildings in town to decorate them.' Ben looked pointedly at Matty and she quickly spoke up.

'We're starting tomorrow. You can help us…although when I say *us*, I mean, *me*. Pauly and Chicco are heading out to Smarter's station. They're the only two other kids who live in this place.'

'Smarter's station?' Thomasena asked, pleased James was being made to feel welcome, although right now he seemed more interested in keeping the flies off himself and watching the ground. She'd give anything to see the weight lifted from his shoulders, to see a real smile back on his face. He'd been through too much at too young an age and she wanted him to feel young and free once more. Hopefully Blaytent Springs was the place where that would happen.

'Big property about three days from here—well, that's walking. About five hundred kilometres.'

'Walking?' She was astounded.

'Yeah, Pauly and Chicco are gonna start off tonight once the sun goes down,' Matty explained.

And these were schoolboys? 'How old are they?'

'Pauly's fourteen and Chicco's fifteen. Aah, don't worry about them.' Matty swatted Thomasena's concern away with the flies. 'They do this most years. Go walkabout. Plenty of people do.'

'O-K, then.' Thomasena's words were hesitant. It was another world. It was the same country she'd lived in all her life yet it was completely different. They walked on, dragging their bags behind them, Matty keeping up a steady stream of chatter.

By the time they entered the main street, Thomasena was perspiring and glad of her hat. She wished for a cold shower and hoped the accommodation they'd been put into at least had a decent supply of water. Her research into the outback had raised her awareness to the plight of water restrictions and the lack of water but she also knew that they had arrived right in the middle of the 'wet.' The outback, she'd read, was hot all year around and had only two seasons—wet and dry. She was surprised to see a mass of green trees in the distance and pointed.

'What's that?'

'That's the springs,' Matty said, before her father could get in. 'That's where we go swimming.'

'Swimming? What about crocodiles?'

'No crocs in there,' Ben assured her. 'The springs are too far from the main waterways. Too much land for the crocs to cover. Safe as houses, Tom.'

She blinked at the nickname, but let it slide. She also

saw a telltale smirk hovering around his lips and realised he wanted her to react. Was he trying to test her? Test her patience? Well, she wouldn't give him the satisfaction. She'd been well trained in the art of controlling her temper. Nice young ladies *never* lost their temper and she was a nice young lady, if nothing else.

Instead, she asked Matty, 'So what year have you just finished at school?'

'Year nine.'

'She's ahead of the rest of her class,' Ben explained with fatherly pride.

'Well done.'

'I've just done year nine, too,' James piped up, and Thomasena was impressed. Her son wasn't one to recommend himself to strangers but it appeared he couldn't let himself be outdone by a *girl*.

'Really? Another smart kid in our midst.' Ben nodded his approval to his colleague as though he was proud of her for bringing up such a fine young man. Oddly enough, his approval made Thomasena reevaluate her opinion of him yet again. In fact, she decided to stop forming opinions of Benjamin Caruthers and to simply relax and take her new outback experience as it came. At least, she hoped she could do that.

'Do you go to an actual school?' Matty asked.

'Er…yes.' James wasn't sure what she meant.

'What's it like, being around so many other kids?'

'Uh…OK, I guess.'

'We do schooling via correspondence. School of the air. You know, radio and Internet and stuff like that. It's great yet *Dad* wants to send me away to boarding school in Darwin.' She shot her father a dark look. 'I'm not that interested.'

'We can discuss it later, Matilda,' Ben interjected, a little embarrassed his daughter had raised the subject. The two kids continued to chat as they came off the dirt road onto bitumen and Thomasena found herself walking side by side with her new colleague.

'Tell me, Dr Caruth—excuse me, I mean, Benjamin. Do you prefer having different doctors come for six months at a time or are you actively seeking someone for full-time employment here?'

Oh, she was pure charm and elegance. Ben idly wondered how long it would take to knock the edges off Thomasena Bates. 'We've tried advertising for a full-time doctor, Tom, but no one wants to come. Six-month rotations—and sometimes they don't even last that long—are all I seem to be able to fill.'

'Sometimes they're shorter?'

'No. Sometimes the doctors give up and leave.'

'That's hardly professional.'

Ben shrugged. 'What are you going to do, eh? They realise the *real* Australian outback isn't at all the romantic one they see on TV.'

'That's fair enough. From what I understand, it can be quite unforgiving territory.'

'So can the city.'

A smile came easily to her lips. 'Touché. And what about you? Why do you stay out here?'

He blew a fly from his nose. 'You mean, out here in the middle of nowhere?'

'*Nowhere* isn't a place, Benjamin. It's a state of mind.'

He paused for a moment, absorbing her words and nodding slowly. 'Very deep.'

'Thank you. That still doesn't answer my question or are you trying to avoid it by changing the subject?'

'The answer's just not that interesting. I'm an outback boy through and through and, apart from studying medicine in Darwin, this has always been my home.'

'Blaytent Springs?'

'Well, I've been here since graduating but my own home wasn't too far away. Besides, Matty loves it here so why would I ever want to leave?' The question was rhetorical and she nodded.

'So why do you want to send her away?'

'Uh…' He felt a little uncomfortable, broaching such a personal subject with someone he didn't know that well. It was a strange feeling for him as he knew *everyone* in the town and *everyone* knew him. Then he shrugged and decided, why not? There were no secrets out here. 'She deserves to have more opportunities. I'm not saying she should leave right now but perhaps she should board for her final two years of school. They're the important ones.'

'Something to consider.' Thomasena nodded. 'What does Matilda's mother think? Is she of the same opinion?'

He exhaled harshly. 'She doesn't have an opinion. She left when Matty was six. The isolation was too much for her. Not her place, I'm afraid. Last I heard, she was living in Vancouver.'

'Quite a leap from here.'

'What about you? Jimmy's father not in the picture?' He'd already noticed that she only wore one ring and that was a signet ring on her right hand.

'No. He died two years ago.' Usually when she confessed she was a widow, people often made the right remarks such as 'I'm sorry' or 'That must have been difficult for you' or, the worst of all, 'Well, it's better to have loved and lost than never to have loved at all'. Lip service and clichés, all of them, and she would smile politely until her cheeks ached. She didn't see why now should be any different and steeled herself.

Ben looked over at her and nodded. '*Now* your comment about nowhere being a state of mind makes sense. I'll tell you this, though, if you can survive that mental type of nowhere, then this place should be a breeze.' He stopped and pointed to the house in front of them. 'Here we are. That's the clinic there…' He indicated the building next to the house. 'Matty and I live on the other side. That's the general store, tennis court—hope you play because we have a big Christmas tournament on next week.'

'I do, actually.'

'Uh…what else? That's where the vet lives and works— Lottie's her name. You'll meet her tonight. Uh…the police station. Sergeant Chit Orwell in attendance.'

Thomasena raised her eyebrows at the name. 'A local?'

'With a name like that? Nah.' He chuckled. 'Chit's American. New Orleans, to be precise. He's used to busting up brawls—and most of them occur in the pub.' He indicated the largest building on the strip of road. 'You've seen the airport and, well, that's about it. Welcome to Blaytent Springs.'

Thomasena smiled to herself. Her father would go spare, seeing this place. He'd deem it not worthy of his daughter and send a private helicopter to pick them up in the blink of an eye. But this, being here, was nothing to do with her father. For the first time in her life, she was going to stand on her own two feet and take full responsibility.

'I'm sorry, did you say something about tonight? Is something happening I don't know about?'

'We're having a special dinner in your honour…well, yours and Jimmy's. You know, to welcome you to town.'

'We?'

'Everyone.'

'In town?'

Ben chuckled. 'Yep. That would amount to about fifteen of us but a lot of the guys who live and work in the community will be in for a drink at the end of a long, hot day so I reckon we might actually hit about thirty people. Give or take a few.'

'Oh.'

They carried the bags inside and Ben pointed out a few of the 'features'. 'Fan switches are next to the lightswitch in each room, mozzie zappers are in the kitchen under the sink, along with the fly and cockroach spray. All the screens on the windows and doors have been recently replaced so you shouldn't have any problems. If you do, give me a yell and I'll come see to whatever needs doing.'

'Handyman as well as doctor?'

'Well, I am a man and I'm handy to have around, yeah,' he confirmed with a cheeky grin, which made her knees go weak. 'Guess you could call me that.'

Thomasena shook her head. 'Are you ever serious about anything or is "town larrikin" part of your résumé?'

'Nah. There are plenty more larrikins about than just me. The pub at six o'clock,' he said as he and Matty walked out the door. 'We may even be able to go for a quick dip after tucker.'

'Swim? After dinner?'

'The sun doesn't set until well after eight o'clock at night at the moment. Pub. Six o'clock. Don't be late and, aah…' He grinned at her. 'Don't get lost.' With that, her new colleague and his daughter were gone.

Thomasena let out a sigh and turned to survey her surroundings. The furniture was a mix-and-match-type thing with the lounge producing a very 1970s feel, whilst the dining-room table was art deco. The table lamps had pictures of cute and fuzzy bunnies on them and the bookshelf was made out of crude timber, giving it a very rustic feel. Still, it was furnished and would no doubt do for their six-month stay.

'Which bag did my computer end up in?' James asked.

'Computer? Already?'

'Mum.' He shook his head. 'Don't start. I'm a teenage boy—'

'Almost,' she interrupted.

'Mothers aren't supposed to understand teenage boys.' James had been checking the luggage labels as he spoke and when he finally found the one with his name, he took it and one of the backpacks into his room.

'Do they even have Internet access out here?' she called after him.

'There was a satellite dish on the roof of the pub and Matty told me they get broadband,' he returned. Thomasena headed up the corridor, her shoes echoing on the wooden floorboards.

'What do you think of the place?' she asked, managing to stand in his doorway before he had the chance to shut her out. He was too polite to close the door in her face.

James shrugged. 'It's OK.'

'Matty seems nice.'

He shrugged again. 'She's a girl.'

Thomasena's lips twitched. 'Glad you noticed.'

As though James realised he wasn't going to get away from his mother that quickly, he rolled his eyes then said, 'The town looks good. Matty's OK for a girl and her dad's pretty cool—except he needs lessons in how to button his shirt properly.'

'Thank you, darling.' She reached out a hand and

brushed it over his hair, trying not to feel a little hurt when he edged backwards. 'I'll leave you in peace now.'

'Thanks.' James went to shut the door.

'Although, please, unpack your clothes.'

'Yes, Mum.'

Thomasena shook her head and walked back through the house, going into the kitchen and opening cupboards and drawers. She looked at the phone on the wall, also *circa* 1970s, and knew she should call her father. No. She didn't have to check in. She wasn't an employee...not anymore. Her mother would worry, though.

Frowning, she lifted the handset to check whether or not the phone was connected and when she received a dial tone, her fingers hesitated over the number she knew far too well.

'No.' Returning the receiver, she decided to get settled in first. It didn't take more than half an hour to unpack so she had a quick shower, pleased to finally change her clothes. They'd been travelling since very early that morning, having flown from Sydney to Darwin where they'd had to wait around for a few hours before boarding the small plane which had brought them here to their new home. Blaytent Springs.

Not sure what to wear to the pub, she decided on something bright and summery, which definitely fitted the surroundings. The skirt she'd purchased on a last-minute whim yesterday would do perfectly and she donned the floral skirt, which came to midthigh, and teamed it with a light blue sleeveless top that matched the colour of her eyes. She combed her wet black hair, surprised to find it drying rapidly, and pulled it back into a simple ponytail, clipping it in place with an artificial lily. Slipping her feet into a pair of flat leather shoes, she surveyed her appearance and was quite satisfied with the result.

Sighing, she knew she couldn't put the inevitable off any longer and walked back to the phone in the kitchen. Picking up the receiver, she dialled her parents' home number, praying silently that her mother would answer. Not having to speak to her father right now would be a big relief.

'Hi, Mum. It's me,' she said into the receiver a moment later, and slumped onto the stool beside the phone. 'We're here.'

'Oh, thank goodness, dear. Is it hot?'

Thomasena smiled. 'Yes, Mum, but, then, we knew it would be.'

'And James?'

'He's fine. He's already on his computer, surfing the net.'

'They have Internet access there? My word. That's very up to date of them. Well, I'm glad you arrived safely, dear. Here's your father.'

'No—Mum…it's…'

'Thomasena?'

'Hello, Dad.'

'When did you arrive?'

'Not long ago.'

'I'm surprised you survived the flight.'

'Thank you.'

'Aeroplanes that small shouldn't be allowed to fly. Disgraceful.'

'It was perfectly safe, as are we.'

'But for how long? You have no business taking my grandson out into the middle of the outback.'

'I disagree. James is fine.'

'There are so many dangers out there. Crocodiles, red back spiders, white tails, funnel webs. Australia has the highest number of deadly and poisonous animals or insects in the world.'

Thomasena forced herself to breathe as she pulled the phone away from her ear. It wasn't the first time she'd heard this and no doubt it wouldn't be the last. She waited for him to run out of steam, waited for him to finish berating her decision-making process before she reiterated what she'd said to him the last time they'd spoken.

'I understand the dangers, Dad—'

'If you honestly do understand them, you wouldn't have made this foolhardy decision in the first place. What were you thinking?'

Of getting away from your overbearing influence, she thought. 'James is old enough to understand the dangers, is mature enough to learn what to do if things do go wrong. If he'd been any younger, of course I wouldn't have come, but it's going to be a good experience for both of us.' And they had the chance to witness the rich Australian beauty firsthand. Even walking into town, Thomasena had been awed at the vibrant colours—the reddy-oranges, the mix of greens from the trees, all blended with the clear blue of the cloudless sky.

She could feel the anger, the oppressive atmosphere her father always created within her starting to rise to the fore. She wished she could let go, to yell, to scream, to bellyache, to get her frustrations out—but it simply wasn't her. As the tears started to build, Thomasena clenched her teeth but kept her voice polite as she interjected, 'Anyway, I need to go. Just wanted to let you know we'd arrived safely. Bye.' And with her father still blustering on, Thomasena returned the phone to the cradle. She sniffed, brushing away the tears that blurred her vision with the back of her hand.

'Still going on, is he?' James asked, and she turned quickly.

'I didn't hear you.' He'd obviously showered as well as his hair was still slightly damp and he was now dressed in his swimming shorts with a cotton T-shirt and thongs. 'Yes, that was your grandfather.'

'Biologically, perhaps.'

'James.' She reached out to him but he walked away. Thomasena went after him and placed both hands on his shoulders and turned him to face her. 'Work is his life. You know that.'

'He goes on and on about how you're doing the wrong thing for *his* grandson but he doesn't care about me at all.'

'Just as he doesn't care about me, either. Believe me, I know how you're feeling.'

'Then why do you call? Why bother putting yourself through that pain?'

'Because Grandma would worry.' Thomasena smiled at him. 'Now…ready to go over to the pub for our welcome to Blaytent Springs dinner?'

He shrugged and she dropped her hands. 'I guess.' James pointed to the cuckoo clock on the wall. 'Although, if we go now, we're going to be a bit early. There's no Sydney city traffic to fight out here.'

'I guess not. Well, it won't matter if we're fifteen minutes early, would it?'

'What I don't understand,' James continued, 'is why Ben told us not to be late. All we have to do is walk across the road, and it would be pretty impossible to get lost in this place.'

'That's why he said it, darling. He was joking.'

'Oh.' James smiled sheepishly.

'Tom? Tom?' Matty's voice had her racing for the door to find Ben's daughter hurtling towards her, a piece of tinsel slung around her shoulders like a scarf. 'Tom. Come quick. There's been an accident at the pub and Dad needs help.'

CHAPTER TWO

As SHE raced out into the heat, forgetting her hat and instantly surrounded by flies, Thomasena's mind rushed ahead to different scenarios. 'What happened?' she asked Matty as they stepped up onto the footpath.

'We were hanging the decorations and, well, the ladder overbalanced and…' She trailed off as she opened the large screen doors of the hotel. The bar was down the corridor and already she could hear talking and laughter, mostly male, as the men washed away the day with a few beers. The door they'd come through led to a small area with a desk and computer where travellers could obviously check into the hotel section of the establishment.

It took a moment for her eyes to adjust from the bright sunshine outside but she could just make out a figure sprawled on the floor at the base of a ladder. She rushed over and knelt by the supine form, her face radiating shock when she realised it was Ben who was lying on the floor.

'I'm all right,' he muttered, then glared at his daughter. 'I told you I was fine.'

'So fine you can't move,' Thomasena remarked. 'What did you do?'

'Fell off the ladder. What does it look like,' he snapped,

more embarrassed than hurt. Now he had the gorgeous princess from the city, who was dressed as though she'd stepped from a field of spring flowers and smelled just as sweet, leaning over him.

'Is he going to be all right?' Matty asked, concern evident in her voice.

'Well, his mouth is fine,' Thomasena said, and was rewarded with a chuckle from someone behind the desk. She looked up. 'Hello. I'm Dr Bates.'

'Tom,' Ben contradicted. 'Her name is Tom.'

Thomasena returned her attention to her recalcitrant patient. 'Keep quiet and let your doctor examine you.'

'You're not my doctor.'

'Really? Is there another medical professional in town?' She glared at him as though daring him to contradict her.

'Lottie,' he said after a moment.

Matty snorted at this information. 'She's a vet, dad.'

'Quite so.' Thomasena nodded. 'Shall I call her over to give you a rectal examination, as she would for most of *her* patients who have sustained a fall?' The man behind the desk winced at this, then laughed.

'She's got ya there, Doc.'

'Fine.' Ben knew when he was beaten.

'Fine what?'

'Fine, you can be my doctor.'

'Oh, so gracious…' There was a twinkle in her eyes as she added, 'And quite the handyman, or so I'm told, although with evidence to the contrary, I'm not so sure about calling you to change a light bulb at my new abode.'

'Wow. A doctor and a comedienne. We're really getting our money's worth out of you,' he said sassily.

Thomasena chuckled and Ben closed his eyes at the sound. The woman was beautiful, she smelled wonderful, especially so fresh from her shower, and now the sound of her tinkling laughter washed over him. He knew there was no harm in looking but in the few short hours that he'd known her he'd begun to wonder, and when he began to wonder…well, that's when things started getting out of hand. It was wrong to even think about her in that way. Not only was she simply his colleague, he knew of old that after a few months here in the outback, she would leave—as they all did. Granted, she seemed stubborn enough to stick it out for the term of her contract, but once it was up, she'd take her 'outback experience' and disappear from his world. He'd do well to stop wondering—and now!

Thomasena gently tested his reflexes, looked into his eyes and asked him general questions, all of which he answered like a dutiful patient whilst trying not to commit the scent of her perfume to memory.

'Let's get you up,' she said when she was satisfied with her examination. 'Matilda, fetch a chair. Slowly, Benjamin.'

'Nah. It's cool.' He didn't need her touching him but knew it would seem rude to refuse when she was only trying to help him up. He took a step away, stumbled and leant on the desk. 'I'm OK.' He shifted, as though trying to prove his point, but only ended up wincing in pain.

'Obviously you're not. Still lower back that hurts?' She came around him and was about to touch him in the lower spine region when he moved again, wincing once more.

'It's fine. Bruised coccyx. That's all.'

'I hope that's all but it is the conclusion I've come to. Tell me, do you have X-ray facilities here?'

'One new digital machine, but I don't need an X-ray. A couple of beers should do the trick. Light, of course.'

'No. You should take some anti-inflammatories, not drink alcohol.'

'A beer has been used for many a cure out here, let me tell you,' he began, declining the chair his daughter offered him.

'Is that so?'

'Of course. Beer has been proven to be a cleansing source of silicon which, as you would know from your extensive research into outback life, is essential for healthy bones, which can stop the onset of osteoporosis. Beer is also a good source of vitamins B6, B12 and folic acid.'

'And consuming too much can not only dull pain for a few hours but cause headaches, as well, not to mention irreparable damage to the brain and liver. What good are healthy bones if you have brain damage and cirrhosis of the liver?'

'Hmm.' Ben frowned at her and pointed to the doorway that led to the bar. 'It's been far too long since I've had a medical debate in a bar.' He raised his eyebrows and met her gaze, leaning slightly towards her, and Thomasena tried not to be impressed by his stature, determination and wildly masculine scent. 'I'm gonna go have a beer, despite what you say, *Doctor*.' He grinned and walked gingerly towards the bar, calling for the publican to set him up with a cold one. It wasn't perhaps his finest hour or his finest exit, but he was beginning to enjoy the verbal sparring with Dr Bates far too much. 'No more wondering about "what if?"' he muttered to himself.

'What about the tinsel?' Matty called. 'You said you'd help me.'

'I don't think it's wise for your dad to climb any ladders, at least for the next seven to ten days, Matilda.' Just then she spotted James leaning against the wall, watching everything with serious interest. 'James could help you.'

'What?' The boy pushed himself upright.

'You wouldn't mind helping Matilda with hanging the

tinsel?' she asked, and received a nonchalant shrug for her efforts.

'Suppose.'

'Cool.' Matilda was bright.

After telling both James and Matilda to be careful, she glanced through the doorway into the pub to where her first patient was chatting away with his mates and doing a very good impression of dulling the pain. She shook her head, realising he was a stubborn man. Then again, he was a doctor, and it was often said that doctors made the worst patients.

As she headed back across the road to her new house, she couldn't help but smile as she recalled Benjamin's initial embarrassment when she'd walked in the door with his daughter. Being sprawled out on the floor, flat on his back, probably wasn't the image he'd been hoping to portray to his new colleague. Oh, well, there was nothing to do about it now.

'Coo-ee.' The sound came from her front door and when she went to investigate, it was to find a strange woman standing in her living room. Well, Benjamin had told her they were very informal here. The townspeople probably thought of this building as theirs rather than respecting the privacy of whoever was staying in it. 'G'day. I'm Lin. I'm the receptionist-nurse-type person, general dogsbody at the clinic.'

'Oh. I'm delighted to meet you. I'm Thomasena.' They shook hands.

'Pleased to meet you, Tom.'

Why did everyone insist on shortening her name? She smiled politely. 'Would you like a drink? I'm not exactly sure what's in the refrigerator but I can take a look.'

'I'm sweet.' Lin brushed the offer away. 'And just so you know, you have apple and orange juice, cold milk and cold water. There's no point in putting wine or beer in there with the pub right across the street. Cheaper to buy it from the counter rather than by the bottle over the counter, if you ask me. Besides, drinking alone isn't good. Being with mates in the pub is the best way to end the day.'

'Is that how most days end around here?'

'Oh, yeah. Most definitely, Tom. Me and Chit live just behind the police station.'

'You're married to the policeman from New Orleans?' Thomasena said, remembering the information Benjamin had told her.

'Yep. Roped him good 'n' proper when he came to town. 'Course, I was the only real single girl around but there were plenty coming in from the stations to try their luck with him, but he said he had eyes for no one but me from the instant he arrived in town. Came only for six months—like you—and now he's been here for going on seven years.' Lin smiled. 'So how about you? What's your story?'

Thomasena blinked. 'Sorry?'

'Why did ya come here to the outback?'

'You needed a doctor.'

'Oh, sure, but that's just an excuse. You see, most of the doctors we get here either come because they think it'll look good on their résumé, you know, that they worked in a remote area to help lessen the load on the poor outback general practitioner.'

'I'm not interested in my résumé.'

'No. I don't believe you are but, then again, I've seen your résumé and it's quite healthy, but what I can't figure out is why anyone would stop working at one of Sydney's most prestigious medical clinics. Jobs there are coveted.'

'I felt like a change.' Thomasena shrugged.

Lin smiled. 'Nah. That's not the truth and you may as well tell me because I'm the sort of annoying person who digs and digs until I get the truth.'

'You don't think that's a little invasive? A person is entitled to their privacy.'

Lin threw back her head and laughed. 'Privacy? Out here? Oh, Doc, you *do* have a good sense of humour. You'll fit right in.'

'You don't have any privacy?'

''Course not. So what's the *real* reason? Because I've been trying to figure it out and I can't.'

Thomasena sighed and glanced at the clock. It was almost six—almost—and as she only had to walk across the road, there was no way she could claim an excuse. 'All right. My father owned the clinic. We have a sister clinic in Melbourne, as well.'

'We?'

'He does. He's senior partner.'

'He's a doctor?'

Thomasena nodded. 'Surgeon. When I declared my intentions of becoming a GP, he made sure I worked at the best place in town—so determined that he made sure it was the best place in town by sinking a lot of money into it.'

'Sounds like a fantastic father.'

Thomasena's eyes glazed over with ice. 'I never asked for any of it.'

'Aah. The old overbearing, domineering father act. I get it.'

'Sorry to be so clichéd.'

'Nah, don't sweat it,' Lin said, and the two women laughed. Thomasena decided she liked Lin, liked her straight talking and the roughness that went with it. She wasn't wearing a scrap of make-up and was dressed in shorts and cotton shirt, her reddish gold hair hanging dry and limp around her shoulders. She'd tossed her hat onto the table by the door as she'd come in.

'What about your old ched?'

'I beg your pardon?'

'Your old man? Your husband? Your résumé didn't state your martial status but I'm presuming there's been a man in your life some time in the past, given that you have a young boy.'

'He's almost thirteen and I'm a widow. My husband died two years ago.' She again waited for the platitudes. They didn't come.

'Fair enough. Nearly thirteen, eh? That'd be good for Matty. Good for her to have someone her own age around for a bit. You know, Tom—' Lin gave her a friendly tap on the back, which almost sent Thomasena flying forward '—I think you're gonna do all right here.'

'You think?'

'Sure, and you look right pretty. Very…city.'

Thomasena smiled. 'I'll take that as a compliment, if you don't mind.'

'Oh, no. I didn't mean anything by it. Just your clothes are very different to what most sheilas wear out here.' She indicated her own garb of shorts and T-shirt then pointed to Tom's hat. 'New hat?'

'Yes. I was just going over to the pub.'

'But it's not six o'clock,' Lin said, picking her own up.

'I know, but I thought as I was ready I may as well head over.'

'Ladies' bar doesn't open until six.'

'Pardon?'

'Ladies' bar. It's an old tradition Fitzy keeps in place.'

'Fitzy?'

'The owner of the pub. Dezza owns the hotel section and the two of them are always arguing. Like grumpy old men, those brothers.' She leaned in closer. 'The yarn goes that they fell in love with the same girl thirty years ago. Chased her here and set up shop in the hope that she'd be impressed with them. In the end, she decided on neither of them—place was too isolated for her—and back then it was worse than now—and she left.'

'That's sad.'

'Nah. Fitzy and Dezza are all right. They laugh about it—well, after a few beers.' Lin shrugged. 'Then they fight about it, and I mean *fight*.' She clenched her fists and put them up.

'Interesting. So ladies aren't allowed in the bar until six o'clock?'

'Yep. That's the rule, but we can always go over and sit and chat with Dezza for a bit.'

'Shall we go, then?' Thomasena placed her hat on her head.

'Terrific.' Lin led the way and as they left the house, Thomasena realised there were no locks on the doors. She'd read about that, too. It was strange, though, not needing to lock the place up.

'Tell me, Lin, what sort of crime is there in the area that it requires a full-time police officer? Oh, not that I mean any slight,' she added.

'None taken. Chit breaks up bar fights, deals with stock theft. We have the odd tourist who's a bit shady and decides that as there's not a lot to do here they'll steal from people's houses or the store or whatever. Before Chit came it was worse, but when people see that there's a police presence in the town, it makes all the difference.'

'That's great.'

'Stock theft mainly,' Lin continued as they entered the hotel. 'Those blokes out on the stations can get mighty sneaky, especially if they have a family vendetta against each other.'

'Really? Sounds intriguing.' She looked around the room, surprised that in the short time since James had come over, he and Matilda had transformed it into a Christmas fairytale. 'Lovely.' There was no sign of the man who had been behind the desk before, whom she presumed was Dezza, so the two preteens had obviously done this all by themselves. 'Just lovely.'

'Yeah. I think so, too,' Ben said from the doorway, a beer in his hand. And he wasn't just talking about the room but she didn't need to know that. He was walking with less stiffness than he'd exhibited before.

'I see the beer is obviously doing the job. Helping with the pain?'

'Pain?' Lin asked.

'It's nothing.' Ben swatted the comments away as he would a fly. 'You don't need your hat on inside, Tom,' he said, and before she knew what had happened, he'd flicked it off her head and tossed it onto one of the hooks by the door. 'Ta-dah.'

'Magician?'

'Nah. I just like that pretty little floral clip you're wearing. Very…feminine.'

'Thank you.' Thomasena began to blush under his gaze.

'Aw, isn't this cute? Just like me and my Chit when we met. Love at first sight, that was.'

Thomasena opened her mouth to correct Lin's assumption but the clock in the bar began to strike loudly.

'Beauty. Six o'clock and I'm parched,' she said, pushing past Ben and racing into the bar.

'Um…' Thomasena felt awkward and found she

couldn't look at Ben for a moment. 'I guess we should go on through,' she managed to get out haltingly.

Ben didn't move from his spot near the door. Instead, he just stood there, drained his glass and put it down on the floor next to the wall. 'Are you annoyed with what Lin said?'

His nonchalance and teasing air were enough to make Thomasena look at him. 'What if I am?'

'We're done here. For now,' Matty said, interrupting. 'Tomorrow we'll do inside there.' She pointed to the area of the bar, which was even more populated than before. 'Come on, Jimmy. Let's go get a drink.'

Thomasena opened her eyes wide at this comment and put a hand up to stop both children. 'Excuse me? Where do you think you're going?'

'In there.' Matty pointed.

Thomasena spun around to look at Ben. 'You let her drink beer? She's twelve years old! Do you have any idea what that would do to her body?'

'She doesn't drink beer,' Ben clarified, straightening his shoulders as he spoke. 'And if she *did*...' he levelled a strict paternal glare at his daughter '...she knows the consequences.'

Matty rolled her eyes and sighed. 'If I get caught drinking alcohol without my father's permission before I turn eighteen, I will be forced to wear a dress, high heels and make-up every day until my eighteenth birthday.'

'Exactly.'

'That's a punishment?' Thomasena extended her hand towards Matty. 'She's a *girl*, Benjamin. It's what girls do.'

He chuckled at that. 'Not *my* girl. She's got tomboy written all over her, right, Matty?'

'A dress?' Matty asked with incredulity. 'Can you imagine *me* in a *dress?* I can think of nothing worse...well, except for high heels. They should be banned. They throw out the alignment of your spine, can stretch your calf muscles and give you corns on your feet, not to mention the fact that I've heard they're majorly uncomfortable. No, thank you.' She turned to James. 'Now, are you coming to get a drink of *lemonade* or not?'

He glanced at his mother, who nodded her assent before he followed Matty.

'They are allowed in there,' Ben said. 'Australian law permits it. It's illegal for them to consume alcohol in there but, when accompanied by an adult, they're permitted to go in there.'

'Then we'd best go in.'

'Just a minute.' He put up a hand to stop her. 'I think we need to clear up a few things first.'

'And they are?'

'Don't get embarrassed or worried that people in the town will link the two of us together. We'll be working closely together at times, especially for the first few months. So if, like Lin, they immediately jump to the conclusion that we're a couple, don't let it bother you.'

'Why not? It would be a completely absurd assumption.'

'Why?' He seemed put out by her words.

'Uh…well…' She swallowed, surprised at being put on the spot. All her training, her finishing school, the social occasions she'd attended over the years—nothing had ever been like this. Frank and open discussions weren't a part of her life. She had thought they'd been, but in the past two years since her husband's death, Thomasena had realised that everyone she'd cared about, everyone, except James, had lied to her at one time or another. It was one of the main reasons she'd come out here in the first place. New start. Away from the bosom of her overprotective and powerful family. Away from her colleagues at the family clinic of whom she'd been in charge. Away from the uncomfortableness of her life, to come into the middle of the outback where her colleague of a few hours was now telling her they would inevitably be linked together romantically.

'Yes?' he prompted.

It appeared he wasn't going to let her off the hook. No doubt he was intrigued and amused to find he'd managed to knock her off balance. 'We hardly know each other,' she eventually supplied.

Ben shook his head. 'Doesn't count out here. With so few people to talk to—or talk about—we get to know each other—and each other's business—very quickly. There are no secrets and no pretence, either. What you see is what you get.'

'I see.'

'Do you, I wonder?' He shifted a little closer. 'All I'm saying is, people will link us and the more embarrassed you are and the more you deny it's truth, the more they'll read something into it.'

'So what do you propose I do?'

'Well, for a start, don't use words like propose or they'll be planning our wedding, as well as Christmas.'

'Noted.'

'Just laugh it off. Make a joke.'

'A joke.'

Ben couldn't help smiling. 'You've already made quite a few today, Tom, so I have no doubt you'll be fine.'

'What about the other doctors who have been out here? Have they all been romantically linked to you?'

'I hope not. They were all men. You're the first woman.'

'Aah.'

'Now I think you're beginning to get the picture. Add the

fact that I'm the most eligible bloke in town and you can see why they'll put two and two together and come up with four.'

'Tell me, Benjamin, is it conceit or consensus that leads you to believe you're the most eligible bachelor?'

He laughed at her. 'Neither. Just fact. No. Hold on. I tell a lie. Bertie's single.'

'Bertie?'

'The guy at the airport.' He pointed through to the bar. 'He's over there, knocking back a few coldies.'

'Oh, Bertie. I see.'

'Actually,' he said in a conspiratorial whisper, 'I think you'll be safe from Bertie.'

'Why is that?'

'He's scared of you.'

'Already? I must be doing something right. What do I have to do to get you scared of me?'

'I doubt that's gonna happen, Tom. I'm already highly impressed with you, not only as a medical professional but as a sheila, as well. You've coped quite well for someone who's only been here for a few hours.'

She was surprised by the praise but wasn't sure for a moment whether he was teasing her or not. 'Thank you.'

'I'm not joking,' he said, as though he could read her mind. 'But enough of that. Let's go through and have a drink. You'll be introduced to everyone, probably remember no one's name and be hit on by every bloke, whether married or not.'

'Aah, so there are a few eligible bachelors other than yourself?'

'There are bachelors in there, yes, but I'd question their eligibility if I were you.'

'You obviously think Bertie is eligible.'

'Sure I do. He's under the age of fifty but, then again, you might prefer older men.' Ben shrugged and stepped up to the doorway, waiting politely for her to proceed him. She appreciated the gesture. Was he a gentleman in disguise after all?

'Hey!' someone called from the bar, and both Ben and Thomasena stopped, looking over in the direction of the loud voice. 'Hey, look!'

The noise died down for a split second before a raucous round of applause broke out. There were catcalls and hooting and Thomasena's eyes widened in shock.

'Is this a normal outback welcome or have they started hitting on me *en masse?*'

'No. This is different.' Ben wasn't sure what was going on either until Fitzy called out.

'Kiss her, you fool.'

'What?' Ben's eyebrows hit his hairline. He knew they'd already been grouped as a couple but this was going a little far.

'Kiss her, ya drongo!' someone else yelled. 'You're under the mistletoe.'

Ben and Thomasena both looked up at the plastic mistletoe hung above them in the doorway then stared at each other in total surprise.

CHAPTER THREE

'WOO-HOO, BEN!'

'Way to go, Doc.'

'Caught a right-lookin' beauty there, mate!'

Everyone in the pub was eager for them to kiss and Thomasena felt as though she'd just entered another dimension. What was going on here? Her skin started to tingle with anticipation and fear. He wouldn't kiss her... would he? When it came down to brass tacks, she knew nothing about Benjamin Caruthers, except that he was a divorced father and a clumsy handyman. Surely he wouldn't kiss her.

She swallowed over the sudden dryness of her throat and clasped her hands together, knowing her eyes were probably as wide as saucers. 'What's going on? What is this? Some sort of initiation?' She asked the questions softly, all the while silently pleading with Benjamin to get them out of this situation.

'No. Just getting into the Christmas spirit. Why? Not interested in kissing me, Tom?'

She heard the teasing note in his voice and wondered whether anyone in this town was ever serious. 'Benjamin! I hardly know you and it's not that I'm not interested—'

'Oh, so you are?'

'That's not what I meant and stop putting words in my mouth. I'm not interested in kissing *anyone*. I've been in a relationship once and it turned out awful. I don't need to go back there again.'

'Relationship!' Ben tried not to make more of this than it was. 'It's just a kiss, Tom. One little kiss, not the beginning of a lifelong commitment.' Even as he said the words, Ben's gaze flicked down to the luscious lips, which were parted slightly and quivering. Were they really quivering? Was she really that shaken up by all of this? He looked into her eyes and saw her pain. She was vulnerable—and he felt a stirring deep within him, felt the urge to gather her close and protect her. No. He should walk away. Walk away right now… But he had a room full of yobbos to quell. The noise around them was becoming worse, with people clapping and chanting the word *kiss* over and over.

'Look, we're making mountains out of molehills and arguing semantics. All I can say is that if you're not interested in kissing anyone, then you'd best take care to avoid standing in doorways over the next few weeks.'

'Why?'

'The kids usually put mistletoe up over every single doorway in town.'

'Even houses?'

'You bet. They think it's some kind of wonderful joke to see all the adults kissing each other.'

'But there are only two or three women who live in town, or at least as far as I've seen.'

'Not at Christmastime.'

'What? I don't understand.'

'Aw, stop gabbing and kiss her already,' Fitzy yelled.

'Heaps of families who have lived here or in the surrounding communities come back for Christmas,' Ben continued, as though the barman hadn't said a word. 'Plus there's other family members who have left, like Fitzy's son and Lottie's kids and people like that. They all come back.'

Was this his plan? Was he just going to stand here and talk to her so everyone else in the pub got bored with their conversation and went about their own business? Thomasena began to relax a little and leaned against the doorjamb. 'Why do they come back?'

'To see their families. Don't you do that for Christmas? All get together around a table filled with rich food and stuff yourselves silly?'

'This is boring,' a bloke yelled, and the clapping and chanting died down. 'Fitzy, give me another beer.'

It seemed as though Ben's plan was working. Just a bit longer and they'd be off the hook, although she would take his advice and watch her comings and goings in and out of doorways during the next few weeks. 'Obviously not this year. How about you? Do you have family coming?'

'Nah. It's just me and Matty. Everyone here in the town is family to us.' As though he'd decided that was enough chit-chat for the moment, he straightened to his full height of six feet four inches. 'Ready to get this over and done with?'

Uncertainty flooded back into her eyes and Ben shook his head, knowing he needed distance from her. Several people had turned away, having lost interest, but many were still watching them.

'What? You're still going to—'

'Relax, Tom. Trust me.' He winked at her and took both of her hands in his. Breathing out slowly, he raised them to his lips and pressed a light kiss to each one, before rubbing his thumb tenderly over the spot in a gentle caress.

The action was enough to take her breath away and

her eyes reflected her pleasure in the romantic and gallant gesture. Her knees began to weaken and when he glanced at her she knew her eyes reflected not only surprise but something more...something strange and powerful, something she'd never felt before. An awareness of just how strong, how close and how male Ben really was.

'Welcome to Blaytent Springs, Thomasena,' he murmured, his breath fanning her skin, causing her to tingle all over. In the next instant he'd dropped her hands and walked over to the bar, accepting the beer Fitzy handed him.

'Traitor.'

'Unfair.'

'Do-over.'

'That's not a *kiss.*' The bar erupted with boos and hisses but thankfully it all seemed to be directed at Ben rather than herself. She glanced over at him and watched as he knocked the head off the beer and laughed at something the publican had said. Ben didn't look at her, didn't glance in her direction, and she was left feeling shaken and exposed.

'Over here,' Lin called, and Thomasena was relieved to have someone come to her rescue. 'Take a load off,' Lin continued, and called her husband over. 'What would you like to drink, Tom?'

Thomasena cleared her throat. 'Something long and cool,' she said, after being introduced to Chit.

'Something long and cool coming up, Doc.'

'Oh, and nonalcoholic.'

Chit nodded, understanding completely. 'Coming right up. Y'all just sit on down here with my beau-tiful wife and I'll take care of it.' His American accent—he was from the South, she noted—washed over her and she couldn't help smiling.

'His accent still gets me right here,' Lin said, touching her heart. 'Chit doesn't drink alcohol, either. Out here he's always on duty and you never know when disaster might strike. It's not so bad now, of course. Now that the rains have come, but I tell ya, Tom, that before that drought breaks, I think we all go a little mad.'

'So I've read.' Thomasena shifted in her chair, glancing over at the bar where Ben seemed to be deep in conversation with Bertie. He had one dusty workboot on the footrail and one elbow on the bar, giving his friend his undivided attention. She was grateful that he'd decided to kiss her hand instead of forcing her into a real kiss, but what she hadn't been prepared for was the way her body was still reeling from his tender touch. She didn't even want to contemplate how she'd be feeling now if he'd actually pressed his mouth against hers! Thomasena cleared her throat, pushing the thought right out of her mind and wishing Chit would hurry up with that long cool drink. She was in danger of overheating and it had nothing to do with the weather.

At least James seemed to be slowly opening up and enjoying himself. He was standing by a pinball machine, watching Matty play. After a moment she stepped aside to let him have a turn and Thomasena relaxed a little more when her son accepted the invitation. He was guarded when it came to new people but hopefully, as there weren't many people about in this place, he'd get used to everyone quite quickly and settle down.

When Chit returned with her drink, which was in a long glass and looked like a sunset, complete with little cocktail umbrella through a piece of fresh pineapple, she offered to pay. 'Not tonight, Doc. This here is your welcome party so don't you fret over payin', ya hear?'

'Thank you, Chit. Well, it's certainly very pretty.'

'It's called a surf-coast-sunset. Lin here loves 'em and they're nonalcoholic.'

During the next few hours she had her drink refreshed many times as people came over and introduced themselves. Food was placed out along the bar and everyone could help themselves to the tasty tucker. Ben didn't venture her way at all, although she'd caught him looking in her direction a few times. Each time he'd simply smiled or raised his glass to her in a salute, but he hadn't made any move to come and chat some more.

Usually Thomasena liked meeting new people—after all, she'd been well schooled in the art of small talk—but tonight all she wanted was to get to know Benjamin better. To sit down and talk with him, to find out what made him tick. She wondered why he'd chosen medicine. He certainly didn't look like a doctor. In fact, if a person walked in right now they'd think he was another farmer or rancher, or whatever they called them out here. Just one of the blokes with his mismatched buttoned shirt.

Ben obviously didn't think himself above anyone else, as her own husband had. 'We're doctors, Thomasena,' Walter had said on more than one occasion. 'We've had more training, we know how to deal with a multitude of life-and-death situations, and therefore it's only right that others look up to us.'

At the time she hadn't wanted to argue with Walter but his words had sounded suspiciously like they'd come out of her father's mouth. In hindsight, she realised that the two men—the two men she'd counted on for everything during her life—had been cut from the same cloth.

She wasn't relying on them now. No, sir. She'd taken

the plunge and was now standing on her own two feet. Standing firmly…except for the way Ben made her feel.

At half past eight, she was thinking about calling it a night, having had a long day, when Fitzy sounded a small gong which stood at one end of the bar. 'Attention!' he shouted, and slowly the noise died down.

'I hope everyone's had the opportunity to welcome the new doc to the area.' He gave her a wave and she smiled. 'I know many of you have been up here buying her drinks, so good on ya. Keep spending yer money. I have no objection. Anyways, now that the doc and her boy, Jimmy, are here, we can get the secret Santa under way.'

'The what?' Thomasena asked softly, looking at Lin for an explanation.

'Fitzy will explain.' It was a deep, male voice that spoke from the other side of her and tingles automatically flooded up and down her body.

'Benjamin,' she whispered, and turned to see him pulling up a chair to sit—gingerly—beside her. 'How's your back? Beer doing the trick?'

'And then some.' He grinned, leaning a little closer so she could hear him. She wished he hadn't as his warm breath fanned across her cheek as he spoke. 'Thanks for caring.'

Thomasena tried to calm her fluttering nerves down, trying not to be so thrilled at his nearness. 'I'm your doctor, remember? It's my job to care.'

'Of course it is.' His voice was soft, intimate as Fitzy talked on at the bar. His eyes met hers and neither of them spoke for a moment. 'So…aah…enjoying yourself?'

'Yes, but getting tired.'

'This won't be much longer.'

'OK,' Fitzy said, and banged the gong again as people had started to talk. 'Everyone's name has been written down. We put them into the hat here…' He whipped a hat off Bertie's head and received objections about people having to put their hands into Bertie's stinking and smelly bush hat.

'Wait a sec,' Ben called, and rose to his feet, walking carefully into the hotel section and returning a moment later with Tom's new hat. 'Use Tom's. It's brand spanking new and should it have any odour, it would be far more pleasant that Bertie's.' His comments received a round of laughter and with a wink at Tom he handed her hat over to Fitzy. That was the second time he'd winked at her and she wished he wouldn't. It was creating far too much havoc with her equilibrium.

'Right.' The publican put the little bits of scrunched-up paper into the hat. 'Pass it around. Everyone take one. If ya get someone ya don't wanna do, you've gotta swap with someone else, but make sure you don't give away who ya have until after the swap. If ya get yer own name, put it back 'n' pick again. Yeah?'

'We know the rules, you moron,' Dezza said, taking the hat and withdrawing a name.

'Then what happens?' Thomasena asked Ben, as the hat slowly did the rounds of the pub.

'You've gotta get a gift—no more than ten bucks—or do something nice for them, like clean their gutters or something, and then on Christmas Day some time, you've gotta get it to the person without them knowing. In the evening, when all the presents have been given out, we have a big reveal where you have to go find the person and say you were their secret Santa.'

'Where do you buy gifts from here?' As far as she knew, there was only one general store in town and she wasn't exactly sure what it stocked.

'We do have broadband here so Internet ordering is

usually the way to go. The plane comes in two, sometimes three times a week—especially around Christmas. Otherwise, people are quite creative either in their thinking or they make something. We're all quite…crafty.' He waggled his eyebrows up and down as though he knew some special secret, but Thomasena wasn't sure she wanted to hear it.

When it was her turn, she took a name out of the hat and opened it and saw Matty's name written there. Now, that should be easy but it would require a little thought. What could she get for a twelve-year-old girl who wasn't too thrilled at being a girl?

Ben took a name out of the hat and slipped it into his top pocket. 'Aren't you going to look at it?' she asked.

'Nope.'

'How do you know it's not your name?'

'Because Lottie over there has my name.'

'How can you possibly know that?'

'Because I was watching her. She always takes the piece of paper out, reads the name and then can't stop staring at the person whose name she has.'

'Oh. So should I be looking for someone staring at me?'

Ben smiled at her. 'That wouldn't give you any clues, princess. Half the men in here are looking at you, probably wishing they *were* your secret Santa.'

'Don't say things like that.'

'Why not? It's the truth.'

'It makes me feel highly self-conscious.'

'There's no need to be uncomfortable, Tom. You're a gorgeous woman, like a breath of spring in the heat of summer. What man in his right mind *wouldn't* appreciate that?'

She was touched by his words. 'Well…thank you,

Benjamin.' She twirled the umbrella from one of her drinks, unable to look at him for a moment.

'You haven't been given many compliments in your life, have you?' he stated, watching her closely.

Thomasena wasn't sure how to answer that so instead she rose to her feet. 'I think I'll call it a night. I'm rather tired after all the travelling.' She smiled at the people at their table, her gaze encompassing them all, but she left Benjamin to last and when she did finally look at him she realised he was also standing.

'No chance of a swim? Don't feel like it?'

She shook her head. 'Not tonight, but thank you for the offer.'

'I'll walk you home.'

She laughed at that. 'It's really not that far and it's not as though I'd get lost. In fact, it's not even dark.'

'Still, outback manners and all that.' Then he turned to the rest of the people. 'Tom's leaving,' he announced to the bar in general. There was a chorus of ''Night Doc', ''Night, Tom' and other various words of farewell. The only objection she heard was from her son who was, according to Matty, on a high-score game of pinball and looking forward to a swim.

'Jimmy can't go now. It'll ruin everything,' Matty wailed.

'Why don't you let him stay until the end of the game and then I'll send him on home? There'll be plenty of time for swimming in the morning,' Ben suggested. Thomasena bristled and clenched her teeth, not liking that he was telling her what to do with her son. Then she forced herself to calm down. Benjamin wasn't her father, or her husband, and what he was offering was only a suggestion. She knew if she'd told James right then and there that he was to leave, he would. She also knew he'd be angry with her and no doubt sulk about it for a few days, and that was the last thing either of them needed. The move to Blaytent Springs was supposed to be a new beginning for them and she didn't want to start it off on the wrong foot. Besides, they weren't in Sydney now and they'd only be separated by a road—a road which would have no traffic coming through at this time of night. He'd be safe.

'The moment you're finished, you are to come home. You can swim in the morning,' she told her son, who didn't take his eyes off his game lest he should break his concentration.

'Yes, ma'am.'

'All right. I'll see you soon.' She walked out and was surprised to find it still quite warm outside, although it was cooler than when they'd first arrived.

'That was interesting,' Ben commented as they stepped down onto the road.

'Excuse me?'

'Watching you war with yourself. Very protective of your son, aren't you?'

'And you aren't of your daughter?'

'Of course. Then again, I guess life is different here from in the city. Different dangers.'

'You can say that again. We don't have crocodiles in swimming holes or water snakes, either. The poisonous spider situation is also not as bad as it is out here.'

'You also have a higher rate of crime, break-ins, domestic violence and too much traffic to contend with. In my opinion, that's far worse than the danger of a croc.'

'Interesting perspective.' They were at her house already and she stopped at the door. 'Thanks for walking me home.'

'What? I don't get asked in for a cuppa? Ya know, tea might be just bonza for me poor ol' back, Doc,' he joked, adopting a broader Australian twang, which made her smile.

'If I invite you in, wouldn't that only add to the speculation about us? People would definitely talk.'

'True. The chins are already wagging and no doubt they're all peeping out the windows over at the pub, watching us.' He turned and waved and they could see Bertie waving back. Both of them laughed.

'Lin said there was no such thing as privacy in this town.'

'She's right. Best get used to it sooner rather than later.' He opened her screen door and disappeared inside, returning a moment later with two of her dining-room chairs. Thomasena quickly took them from him.

'Give them to me. You'll do your back further damage.'

'It's all right, Tom. I've got the cutest little doctor looking after me.'

She felt herself begin to blush at his words and turned her head away, hoping he wouldn't see her embarrassment.

'Anyway, it's not as though I haven't bruised my coccyx before. I know what I'm capable of.' He gestured for her to sit. 'Let's watch the sun go down.'

They sat in silence for about ten minutes, Thomasena noting the decrease in flies as the heat started to ebb. 'It's beautiful.'

'Yep.'

'I never got the chance to watch the sunset all that often.'

'Busy stuck inside a hectic medical practice?'

'Yes. I was the senior partner…well, in a way. My father owned the practice but left me to run it.'

'Did you enjoy that?'

'To an extent. My husband used to work there with me and handled the management, but after his death I took over, even though my father objected for a time.'

'It wasn't easy? After your husband's death, I mean?'

Thomasena breathed in and slowly exhaled. 'No. James

was ten and, honestly, I wasn't at all sure what to do. We moved back to my father's house and that's where we've been living for the past two years.' She shook her head. 'In hindsight it was definitely the wrong thing to do.'

'Aah, yes, hindsight. Don't we just love it?'

'I take it you've made mistakes, then?'

'Believe it or not.' He chuckled good-naturedly. 'In fact, I made one tonight.' The tone of his voice had changed.

'You did?' Why had she instantly become aware of just how close his chair was to hers? He smelled of earth and heat and she had to admit it was a heady combination. There was no polish, no expensive cologne, no tailored suit for Benjamin. He was simply an honest, hardworking man, providing medical care for people in an isolated area. Still, her awareness of him as a man seemed to be increasing.

Ben turned his head to look at her. 'Yes. When I kissed your hand.' He exhaled slowly and looked back at the reddish gold sky before them.

The question was on the tip of her tongue but she wasn't sure she could ask it. Her heart started to pound wildly against her chest and her breathing became erratic. 'Why was it a mistake?' she finally choked out.

Ben stood and stretched his arms up, grabbing the roof of the veranda, his back to her. 'Because now I want more.'

'More?' The word was a squeak of surprise.

He looked at her over his shoulder and she saw a smile touch his lips. He was roguishly handsome and she knew he knew it.

'Why wouldn't I? What man could resist you?'

Thomasena looked away and hugged her arms around her as the tingles were replaced with a coolness from deep within her. 'You'd be surprised.'

'Really?' He turned properly to face her, watching her for a long moment. 'Your husband? He rejected you?'

'It was a long time ago now. That part of my life is over.'

Ben noticed that she didn't deny it. So *that* was what she was running from, that and what sounded to be a repressive father. No wonder she'd needed to get out of the city. He nodded. The outback would heal her...if she let it.

'Good. No looking back. That's my motto, too.'

'But you were just reflecting on the moment when you kissed my hand.'

'That's correct. Reflecting is different from looking back, Tom. Reflecting can mean that I'm not at all sure I did the right thing.'

'You did the only thing you could do—short of walking away.'

'And I wasn't about to do that and when I say I'm not sure I did the right thing, I mean, I should have given you a proper kiss.'

'Oh!' The word slid out on a breath, her eyes wide with alarm. She wasn't at all sure what to say. What was the protocol for this type of thing? She doubted there was one. Rising to her feet, she took a few steps towards him but he immediately stepped back, coming up against the rail.

'I want more, Tom. The feel of your skin, the scent of whatever it is you're wearing, it's surrounded me and...I want more.'

'Aah...so...aah...' She stopped. She wasn't used to being without words but neither was she used to a man being so open and honest with her. It was nice but it was also scaring the living daylights out of her. 'What...um... do...you—'

'Intend to do about it?'

She nodded.

'I intend to keep my distance.'

'What?' Confusion washed over her. 'But you just said—'

'I know and anything between you and me…' He shrugged. 'It won't work, Tom. We're from different worlds and in six months' time you'll return to your world and that will be that. Besides, we're colleagues.' He skirted towards the steps and went down them backwards. 'Get some rest. We've got a busy day tomorrow. We'll be leaving early for a trip out to Torch-wood homestead.'

'I see.' She didn't, but she was still trying to process everything else.

'Well, it's more like a huge cattle station but it's called a homestead,' Ben continued. 'Immunisations. Tetanus shots. That sort of thing. Most of the jackaroos there aren't up to date and Mr McDonald who runs the farm insists on all his employees being up to date with their medical jabs.'

'Wise.' Thomasena watched his progress as he continued to walk away from her. 'What time will we be leaving?'

'Around seven-thirty. You'll be up. You won't be able to sleep through the heat by then. Matty and I will be going for a dip at the springs around six-thirty if you or Jimmy want to come with us.'

'Oh, and what about James? What is he supposed to do while I'm off giving injections to jackaroos?'

'Bring him along. Matty tags along with me all the time.' He grinned. 'Advantage to being your own boss.'

'All right, then. We'll be ready to go by seven.'

'Great. And, uh…you might want to pack a bag.'

'A bag?'

'Of clothes and overnight stuff.'

'Why?'

'Hmm…probably because we'll be staying away overnight. There's another clinic at a different homestead on the day after tomorrow so we'll be camping out tomorrow night.'

'Camping?' Her eyes were wide with incredulity.

'You'll be quite safe, Tom. I wouldn't let anything happen to you. I promise.' He crossed his heart and saluted, his grin so cheeky she wasn't at all sure whether he was pulling her leg or not. 'Here comes Jimmy. You get some sleep now, Dr Thomasena Bates. You'll be needing your rest to keep up with me tomorrow.'

With that, he turned and walked back across the road, stopping to shake James's hand and ruffle the boy's hair. Thomasena heard her son laugh and was astonished at his reaction to Ben.

She stood there for quite a while after James had gone inside. She listened to the sounds of the outback, the insects, the faint noise of the patrons at the pub. She took in the surroundings, the way the stars were appearing in the sky, and as she did, she thought of Benjamin Caruthers, of what had happened since her arrival here in Blaytent Springs and of what he'd just confessed. The man wanted to kiss her. For so long she'd felt undesirable, unworthy and unloved.

She was here to have new experiences. Here to shake off the old Thomasena—to find herself. She was on a voyage of self-discovery and now a handsome and intelligent man was not only attracted to her but wanted to kiss her. It didn't even seem to matter that he didn't intend to do anything about it. In fact, she agreed with his reasons for not pursuing it.

For the first time in years she wasn't going to fight herself. For the first time in years she was going to let loose. For the first time in years she was going to enjoy herself.

CHAPTER FOUR

THEY were up bright and early, James heading off to enjoy a morning swim with Matty and Ben while Thomasena went over to the clinic to talk to Lin. The receptionist gave her a run-down on the patients and what she could expect.

'And watch out for Jacko. He's the biggest larrikin of the lot.'

'More so than Benjamin?'

'You'd better believe it.'

Armed with everything they would need, especially the medical supplies, they were out on the road before seven-thirty. James and Matty sat in the back of Ben's four-door ute, watching a DVD on Jimmy's laptop computer.

'I can't believe it's so hot already,' she remarked, pleased Ben had turned on the air-conditioning.

'You should have come for a swim this morning. Very refreshing.'

'Too nervous.'

'Nervous? About what?'

'First day on the job nerves?'

'Nah. No need for them. Just relax and enjoy yourself, although if you think the humidity is bad now, wait until you see the rain. It's amazing. It's almost like clockwork.

See those clouds over there—the cumulonimbus—you'll find almost the same group of clouds in the same place most days. Then, as though the Creator has called "Action", they open up and the rain comes down in buckets. It's really quite spectacular.'

'And this happens every day?'

'Yes. We may get a few deluges here and there but the main rainfall is around four o'clock each day. You just missed it yesterday. It's the main reason the flights to Blaytent Springs only arrive late afternoon.'

'Are they electric storms?'

'Sure. We get our fair share. They're as majestic as anything you're likely to see anywhere. Magnificent.'

Thomasena smiled. 'You make it sound so appealing, I can hardly wait.'

'Really?' Ben glanced at her.

'Sure. It's one thing to do research on a place but quite another to experience it.'

Ben nodded slowly, still amazed that Tom actually seemed to like being there. Then again, it had been less than twenty-four hours and she might well change her mind by the time they returned to Blaytent Springs some time tomorrow.

'What's first on the list today?' she asked, breaking his thoughtful silence. 'You said last night that we were headed out to Torch-wood. Sounds intriguing.'

'Yes. The story goes that the original homestead had been built by old Mr McDonald on his arrival in the outback from Scotland. First of all, though, he'd visited the goldfields down at Ballarat and made his fortune. When he arrived, he built the place out of raw timber but the design was a strange one. The homestead was three storeys but each storey was smaller than the one below it. Up top,

Mr McDonald, not completely trusting the locals, built a sort of lookout tower.'

'Sounds like the tiers on a wedding cake.'

'Exactly. One night, though, the place caught fire and went up in a powerful blaze.'

'It looked like a torch, I'm guessing.'

'Yes.'

'Did everyone survive?'

'One of Mr McDonald's children died in the fire.'

'How did it start?'

'No one's sure. It was during the dry and the Scotsman did have a few enemies here and there.'

'Intrigue?' She raised her eyebrows.

'Yes. Anyway, after that it was referred to as Torch-wood and the name simply stuck. The property has changed hands over the years but now is back with the McDonald family.'

'I guess people either love it or hate it out here.'

Ben nodded, wondering which one Tom would turn out to be. He hadn't been able to stop thinking about her even though he knew it wasn't going anywhere. He'd been kicked to the ground before by a woman—and then when he'd been as low as he could get, he'd been kicked some more. City women didn't mix with outback doctors. That's just the way life was and if he couldn't learn from his own mistakes then he was more of a drongo than he'd thought.

Besides, his first priority was to Matty. He needed to provide for her and while financially he had no concern about doing that, on an emotional level he was discovering they had less and less in common. She'd be a teenager soon and he knew puberty was already starting to take its course. He could explain things to her, the changes to her body and the reasons behind it, but he'd never fully understand because he wasn't a woman. Simple as that.

He checked his rear-view mirror. Matty and Jimmy were sitting in the back with headphones on, their eyes glued to the computer monitor.

'Technology certainly makes travelling these long distances more bearable,' Ben commented, and Thomasena looked at the preteens in the backseat, both engrossed in what they were watching.

'They seemed to have bonded quite quickly.'

'Matty bonds with everyone quickly. It's who she is.'

'James doesn't. He's always had difficulty making friends at school. It never seemed to bother him, though, or not that he told me.' She laughed without humour and shook her head. 'I feel so…out of depth with him all of a sudden. It's as though he's growing into a man but as I'm a woman I have no idea what that entails and therefore can't help him much.'

'That's…scary.'

'What? Not bonding with my son?'

'No. I was just thinking the same thing about Matty— although obviously the reverse in her case.'

'Oh, I see. Well, if you ever need any female advice, let me know.'

'You'd be the expert,' he stated.

'And you'd be the expert on male advice, although I have to tell you that I might not be that good at taking it.'

'Advice or interference?'

She sighed. 'The latter.'

'There's a story there.'

'Yes.'

When she was silent he prompted, 'Come on. I told you a story so now it's your turn. It'll be another hour before we reach the homestead.'

'You told me a story about someone else's home burning down. That was hardly personal, Benjamin.'

He laughed. 'True but, still…share. It'll all come out eventually. Remember? No secrets in the outback.'

'Surely there would have to be a few secrets lying around? Covered with dust, no doubt.'

'Everything out here is covered in dust and quit stalling. All right, I'll share, too, but you go first. Why don't you like interference?'

'Well, the obvious reason would be that I've endured too much of it.' Her sigh was heavy and gave him an indication of just how badly she'd been hurt. 'My father, as I mentioned last night, isn't a man you say no to. I guess you could say I was born with a silver spoon in my mouth, never wanted for anything, the best schools, the best tutors. It was deemed that I should go to medical school like my father and my grandfather. My mother had been a nurse before marrying and my two brothers are both surgeons.'

'A medical family.'

'Quite. When it came time for me to specialise, I couldn't decide and finally realised that general practice would suit me better. I dreaded telling my father but as it turned out, he hadn't *expected* me to train as a surgeon. I was a woman, after all.'

'There are plenty of female surgeons,' Ben felt compelled to point out.

'Yes, but none of them are my father's daughter. Anyway, it turned out best for everyone, although it left me feeling as though I was less than satisfactory in his eyes. However, not long after that, I met my husband.'

'Did your father approve?'

'He introduced us.'

'Arranged marriage?'

Thomasena shrugged. 'I'll never know because I fell in

love. I was the bride with stars in her eyes and within twelve months I was pregnant with James.'

'Did you stop work?'

'No. I worked part time, just a few days a week, at the practice. I could have done more but I didn't like leaving James with nannies. I was his mother and therefore I would raise him.'

'No one to interfere.'

'That's right. Walter was more than supportive of my decision to be with James, even though he spent little time with him. That's beside the point.'

Ben silently disagreed, wondering if that was the reason the boy was so closed off.

'Everything seemed fine for years. Then when Walter was killed, I…well, I fell apart.'

'And rightly so. It happens, Tom.'

'I know, but from then on, everything got worse.'

'Let me guess. Your father stepped in.'

'Yes. He said the best thing was for James and I to move back to his home—which is quite large so we all had plenty of room. However, when I started pulling myself together again, I found I was trapped.'

'Yet you obviously found a way to leave or you wouldn't be here.'

'James wasn't happy and he finally broke down and told me as much.' She shook her head, feeling a failure. 'If only I'd been more in tune with him. If only I'd realised sooner just how miserable he was.'

Ben reached out and placed his hand over hers for a moment. 'Don't beat yourself up, Tom. You were grieving the loss of your husband.' A man she'd said she'd fallen in love with. Did that mean she was still carrying a torch for him? Had her husband been her soul mate? Was she the type of woman to only fall in love once and never love again? And why on earth was he thinking these things? He removed his hand and quickly returned it to the wheel.

'The point is,' he continued after clearing his throat, 'you took the step.'

'And came as far away from my father as I could.'

'Regretting it already?'

'No. Look at my son! We've been here less than twenty-four hours and already he's come further out of his shell than any time in the last few years.'

'Cave.'

'Pardon?'

'It's called a cave, not a shell. Men retreat to their caves.'

'What for?'

'Uh…I've never really thought about it. I guess we need to just escape, to think, sort things out. Yeah. That's about it.'

'Do you have a cave?'

'Every guy has a cave.'

'Thank goodness women don't. More dust is the last thing I need.'

Ben chuckled. 'Women have a cave. It's called *shopping*.'

'Oh. I get it. Women have retail therapy and men retreat to a stinky, dusty cave.'

'Correct.'

'Where they sweat and pine and ponder.'

'Yes.'

'While we shop until we drop.'

'Or max out the credit cards.'

'There is that.' She glanced at her son. 'So James is in his cave?'

'I reckon so but he's venturing out, if what you've told me is correct.'

'Well, that's good, then, right?'

'It is. It's good.'

Thomasena nodded, absorbing this new information. 'What about Matty, though?'

'What about her?'

'Well, she's not a girly-girl and so retail therapy wouldn't work for her.'

'I know.'

'So what does?'

'I think that's part of my problem. I have no idea, Tom.' Ben turned off the bitumen road onto what looked to be a dirt track.

'How much farther?' she asked.

'About another thirty minutes.'

'Would you mind going through what we're doing, please? Lin covered a few things but if you wouldn't mind, I'd appreciate it.'

'Need to know what to expect?'

'Yes. I'm not one for surprises.'

'Something else you'll need to get used to. All righty. Are you sitting comfortably? OK, then I'll begin. First off, we'll be doing immunisations. That's the majority of this clinic. Mac's wife is also pregnant with his third child but she's only about twenty-six weeks so plenty of time to go before the baby arrives. She'll need an antenatal check. There will be quite a few people around as those who live in the neighbouring properties will drop by if they have any medical needs. Plus a few of the jackaroos and overseers are married and live with their families on the property, as well.'

'Quite a little community.'

'Basically, yeah.'

'On Old McDonald's farm?' Her lips twitched as she said the words.

'Don't say "e-i-e-i-o" to Mac, whatever you do.'

Thomasena giggled. 'Noted. So what else?'

'Relax, Tom. Just take things one step at a time. You'll do fine.'

'I hope so. I wouldn't want you to be disappointed.'

Ben chuckled. 'No fear of that. You've treated me, remember? You're my doctor.'

'I didn't *treat* you. I gave you advice, which you promptly ignored.'

'I didn't ignore it. I just didn't follow it immediately. You'll be pleased to know I've taken my anti-inflammatories and the coccyx is feeling much better today.'

'Good.'

'Does this mean you've discharged me?'

'I guess it does.'

Both of them were silent and Ben flicked a button and soon the sounds of Christmas music filled the air. 'Best to get in the mood,' he said.

'There's plenty of time, Benjamin. Christmas isn't until the end of next week.'

'Aah, but at the clinic, you'll be expected to be filled with Christmas cheer.'

'Oh. Why?'

'Because it's Christmas! With Mac's wife being pregnant and him tied up with the property, he emailed me, asking for decorations. Matty and Jimmy continue their decorating apprenticeship this morning. You and I are also required to wear Santa hats and I'm highly impressed you've worn a red top. I meant to mention that last night.'

'It was quite by chance, I assure you.'

'We can tie your hair back with a piece of tinsel, as well. That should help with some Christmas cheer.'

'I should have worn my Christmas earrings.'

'You have some?'

'Yes. Last year James bought me a pair of plastic Christmas trees that flash. They're absolutely gorgeous.' And they'd been the best present she'd received that year and they'd only cost a few dollars. Her father had lavished on her a diamond necklace and matching earrings, demanding she wear them to their Christmas celebration rather than the cheap baubles her son had bought. She had refused—and that had been her very first step of defiance. It had been then she'd realised she would rather go against her father's wishes, than break her son's then eleven-year-old heart. James was far more important and her top priority.

'Just remember, though, Christmas cheer. Christmas cheer. Oh, and you might be asked to participate in another secret Santa thing. They do their own out at the homestead. However, all you need to do is say you're already doing the one in town and they'll let you off the hook. By the way, whose name did you pull out?'

'I'm not telling you.'

'Why not?'

'Because it's part of the rules. I gathered it was the "secret" part of the whole affair.'

'Is it someone in this car?'

'I'm not going to say another word about it.'

'Is it me?' He grinned and waggled his eyebrows up and down.

'Benjamin!'

'I'll tell you mine if you tell me yours.'

'*Benjamin!*' She pointed to the road ahead, a large kangaroo bounding across it. Ben didn't lose speed but swerved with practised expertise, the roo stopping for a second before heading off across a field.

'You all right?' he asked, noting she had a hand pressed to her chest and was breathing fast.

'You might have hit it.'

'No. If it had been dusk, I might have. They tend to have the "frozen in the beam of the headlights" syndrome but as my lights aren't on, it was merely interested in what was going on.'

'Does that happen often?'

'Sure.'

'They just jump out of nowhere?'

'You get used to it but you still need to be cautious and careful.'

'Have you ever hit one?'

'Yes, unfortunately, and they really wreck the car.'

'That's a bit callous.'

'It's also the truth. It's part of life out here and why most vehicles have bull-bars fitted to the front grille of the car.'

'But what about the kangaroo?'

'You usually need to put them out of their misery.'

'You kill it?'

'It's the humane thing to do, Tom.' Ben's tone was soft and compassionate. She didn't speak another word, the strains of the Christmas carols wafting over them as they completed the journey.

When they finally arrived at the driveway to the homestead, Thomasena offered to get out of the car and open the necessary gates, which she knew were a fact of life on properties this big. At some junctions there were cattle grids so there was no need for her to step out into the heat. Life was different out here and she had to keep remembering that and not get upset at the thought of a kangaroo being killed because it happened to jump in front of a car.

When the homestead came into view she was highly impressed. It was a large one-level house, ringed by a veranda. No wedding-tier cake house for *this* Mr McDonald. Smaller houses were placed in the distance and so were farm buildings.

'It's quite a large place.'

'Surprised? Mac employs over fifty men. Then there are cooks, staff to clean lodgings et cetera so, yes, it is quite a large place.' As he pulled up outside the homestead, parking in the closest available spot, Thomasena could see people and children everywhere and their arrival was greeted with calls and whistles.

Both James and Matty helped to carry the bags and crates inside. 'What have you got in here?' Thomasena asked as she carried a cardboard box inside the house. Seeing all the dust about the place, she was regretting wearing her white linen trousers. No doubt they'd be a lovely orangy brown by the end of the day. Oh, well, at least she looked Christmassy with her red top.

'The mail and other things such as paper and printer cartridges.' Ben gave a shrill whistle and a few men came around the corner, accompanied by barking dogs. Thomasena had always wanted to be able to whistle like that and wondered if Ben would teach her. Her father and Walter had deemed it highly unladylike but she'd always had a secret yen to learn. 'Give us a hand,' he said to the blokes, and gestured to the box Thomasena was carrying.

'I've got this one,' she said, but it was taken from her nevertheless and carried inside.

'Can't have you putting your back out, as well.' Ben walked past her into the house, a wide grin on his face. They were going to hold their clinic in the living room, which had a door at either end. The furniture had been pushed aside and a sheet was hanging down the middle so they could both see patients at the same time. They each had a little desk with two chairs and a bottle of water with a little Christmas ribbon tied around it. The extra touch made Thomasena smile.

'Would it not be better to use one of the bedrooms?' she asked.

'This is the way Mac prefers it so this is the way it's done. You'll get that side of the room, I'll take this side.' He handed her a medical kit and when she opened it was pleased to discover it extremely well stocked and not only with vials of the immunisation they would be administering today. He placed a notepad and pen on the desk. 'Take notes for every patient you see. Keep them on the pad and Lin will enter them into the medical records when we get back.'

'Fresh sheet of paper per patient?'

'You've got it, Tom. Ready to start?'

'Yes. Oh, where's James?'

'With Matty. Don't worry. She knows the rules. No wandering off. Remain within the homestead at all times. Use your manners, that sort of thing. She'll look after James. Besides, they have decorations to string.'

'Of course. All right, then, let's begin.'

'Hey—almost forgot!' Ben went behind the sheet but returned a moment later with a Santa hat and a piece of tinsel. 'Here you go.' He handed her the hat and then surprised her further by lifting her hair and slipping the tinsel beneath, tying her hair into a low ponytail at the nape of her neck.

His fingers brushed her skin and she trembled at the feather-light touch. He was standing close, so very close she could feel the heat radiating off his body, and although the large homestead had air-conditioning it did nothing to cool her rapidly heating skin, especially when Ben was so near.

'There you go.' His voice was deeper than usual.

'Thank you.' She turned her head to look at him and only then realised how close their mouths were. Her gaze flicked from his eyes to his mouth and back again and she wondered what would happen next. There was no mistletoe here, no crowd of people watching them.

Ben cleared his throat and with superhuman effort took two steps away from her, almost knocking a vase off the shelf behind him. 'Clinic,' he said, as though forcing himself to remember his resolve of the night before. 'We have a clinic to run. Let's get started.' He shoved his own Santa hat onto his head. 'Ho, ho, ho!' Then he disappeared behind the sheet and called his first patient in.

The men came in and after she'd taken their details and a brief medical history, Thomasena administered the injection, making notes of the vial and batch number. Several of them commented on her Santa hat, smiling brightly and flirting with her—until she jabbed their arms with the needle. After that, she was the one smiling as the big burly men skulked back to their jobs.

Once they were done, it was time for lunch and after that she had other people come and see her. One woman brought her four-year-old daughter in for preschool immunisations.

'You're much braver than some of those big men who have been to see me this morning,' she told the little girl.

'Do I get a sweety for being so good?'

Thomasena frowned for a moment and checked her medical kit. 'You should certainly have one, if I can find them. Just a minute and I'll check with Dr Ben.' She walked to the sheet. 'Excuse me, Dr Ben,' she said. 'Do we have any sweets for patients who have been very good?'

'Tom, Tom, Tom. I thought you would have realised now that if you give one of the men a treat, all the others will want one, too.' Ben pulled the sheet back. 'Oh. It's for you, Maryanne. Well, in *that* case, of course we have sweeties.' He went to one of the boxes in the corner, rummaged around for a moment, then pulled out a lollypop. 'There you go.'

'Thank you, Dr Ben,' Maryanne said.

'What lovely manners,' Thomasena praised, and the child grinned happily. 'Well, that's one happy customer. She was ten times better than half the men I've had in here so far.'

Ben chuckled. 'You ain't seen nothing yet.'

'What do you mean?'

'Jacko.'

'Jacko? Lin mentioned him. Who is he?'

'Only the toughest guy on the station.'

'Let me guess. He hates injections.'

'Got it in one. We'll finish up here and then head out to get him before teatime. It's just easier to leave him until last.'

'OK.' Thomasena called her next patient through and was pleased it was Shelley McDonald—mistress of the house and ready for her antenatal check. Ben had brought a portable foetal heart monitor with him and she listened to the baby's heartbeat. 'Sounds good. Strong and healthy. Did you have any problems with your other children?'

'No. Carried both to term, had natural births.' Shelley patted her swollen stomach. 'This one, though, is already impatient to come out. It hasn't stopped kicking all day long. Dave says he's going to be a footballer. I just want a moment's peace.'

'I remember the feeling all too well.' Thomasena laughed.

'Your son and Matty have done a great job of decorating the house. He has a lot of patience does young Jimmy.'

'That he does.' She sighed, thinking how he'd been very patient, waiting for his mother to come to her senses, but all that was behind her now.

Just before four o'clock, Ben came and found her. 'Ready?'

'For?'

'Jacko. I've written out the paperwork and drawn up the injection. Dave's getting him settled outside. This is something you should come and see.'

'Outside? He can't just come in and have his injection like everyone else?'

Ben laughed. 'Dave doesn't want everything in this room smashed to smithereens, Tom. And I'm not exaggerating.'

'He's that feral?'

'When it comes to needles, yes.'

'Why can't we blindfold him?'

'How do you suggest we get the blindfold on him?'

'Oh. It's *that* bad?'

'It is but not to worry. I've done this before.'

He started walking out of the room, leaving her to follow. 'Done what?' she asked, keeping pace with him.

'Roped and hog-tied Jacko just to give him an injection. It was his flu shot.'

'Flu? Out here?'

'Some people are more susceptible than others despite where they live.'

'True. So you're going to wrestle a man to the ground and give him an injection?'

'That's the current plan, although I might get a few of the other blokes to help with the holding-down part.'

'And you're going to do all this with a bruised coccyx?'

They'd just gone down the front steps and Ben

stopped walking, turning to look at her. 'What? Don't think I can?'

'Think you'd be stupid if you did but you haven't listened to my advice so far, so why should now be any different?'

'If I don't give him the needle, who will? The other guys don't know the correct place to administer the dose.'

'Oh, give it here.' She snatched the injection from him and started walking again.

'No. No. Tom, you don't know what you're getting yourself in for.'

'I'll be fine. I can handle my father, which means I can handle anyone.' She'd wanted to challenge herself when she'd decided to move to the outback, not only in her professional life but personally, as well. How hard could it be to give a man a needle?

The humidity in the air was almost sickly but that didn't stop her. However, when she saw the penned area where they'd put Jacko, she came to a halt. He was in one of the yards where they would usually keep an animal, standing in the middle, his workmates lining the outside fence.

'I doubt giving Jacko a needle is the same thing as discussing career choices with your father, Tom. This isn't a mental challenge. It's physical. Highly physical.'

'All the more reason why you shouldn't do it.' She pointed. 'I take it that's him?' Thomasena took off her Santa hat and handed it to Ben.

'Yes.'

'And he's having tetanus?'

'Correct. Do you need a rope?'

'Do you use one?'

'Yes. You'll need to get him secure. Tom, I really don't like you doing this.' Ben placed his hand on her arm and she saw the concern in his eyes.

'Mum?' James was sitting up on the top fencepost, next to Matty. 'Mum you're not going in there, are you?'

'I am, darling.' She was watching Jacko who stood in the centre, feet apart, arms akimbo as though he was defying anyone, especially some tiny female doctor, who would even *think* of taking a go at him.

'He's twice your size.'

'Benjamin has assured me I'll be fine.' She looked at Ben. 'Haven't you, Benjamin?' Tom patted his hand and stepped away, slipping the syringe into her pocket. 'Guess I won't be needing a swab,' she muttered, accepting the rope from Ben's hand.

'Well, if you're determined…' Ben shrugged. 'Go get him, Tom. Show them what you're made of.'

'You think I can do it?' she asked.

'I do.'

A wave of strength pulsed through her and she straightened her shoulders. She could do this. She knew she could but having someone believe in her made all the difference…*Benjamin* made all the difference.

'But, Mum!' James protested.

She turned and walked backwards, looking at her son. 'I can handle this, James. Trust me.' There was a lot of ruckus as she walked towards Jacko, who was now grinning from ear to ear.

'You?' He laughed. 'You're the one who's gonna give me this needle?'

'I am.'

'What's ya name?'

She looked him in the eyes and in that moment began to feel different. She was accepting the challenge and confidence began to flow through her. 'Tom.' And in that instant she realised she was. She wasn't Thomasena

Prentice Bates, only daughter of Sir Ronald Moore. She wasn't Thomasena Bates, the clueless widow of Walter Bates. She was her own person. She was Tom, and acknowledgement of the nickname strengthened her resolve to prove to every man, woman and child watching that she was capable of handling what was thrown at her. 'Now, Jacko, are you going to go quietly and surprise everyone by just standing there and taking it like a man?'

'Nope.'

'Oh. So you're going to squeal like a little girl. How manly of you.' The smile began to slip from Jacko's face as she put the rope down. 'I should warn you, though, I did go to an all-girls school and let me tell you, girls do not fight fair—not fair at all.' With that, she lunged at him, grabbing hold of his arm with both her hands. The action stunned him and he jumped back, trying to shake her off as though she were a rag doll. Tom managed to hang on for a few seconds before she fell to the ground.

Laughter, clapping and concerned calls met her ears. She blocked them all out as she got to her feet. They wanted a show? She'd give them a show! Taking two steps to the right, Jacko moved in the opposite direction. Then they circled each other, like boxers in a ring, before Tom performed two forward flips and then used Jacko's legs as a climbing pole to vault herself up onto his shoulders.

The crowd went wild. Ben grinned from ear to ear, proud of her. A moment later Jacko had managed to flick her off again but she got right back up and tried another attack.

'Jimmy? Has your mum ever done gymnastics?' Ben asked the boy.

'She was school champion.' James straightened up. That was his mum out there. 'I've never seen her do it, though, other than a few cartwheels when she used to take me to the park when I was little.'

'Well, she certainly hasn't lost her touch.'

'Come on, Jacko,' Tom encouraged. 'It hurts less than a mosquito bite.'

'I hate mozzies.'

'But you can't stop them biting you. Come on. Don't make me use the rope.' His eyes widened and she smiled. 'And, yes, I *do* know how to use one.'

'I'm not having the needle!' he ground out between his teeth.

'I beg to differ.' With him still off guard, she did a cartwheel, then dropped down and kicked at the backs of his knees, bringing him to the ground. With the weight of her shoulder behind her, she forced him forward, then sat on his back, withdrawing the needle from her pocket and sticking it in his arm.

The applause was very real and after she'd finished she quickly moved away, capping the needle, hoping she hadn't made Jacko too mad. Instead, the big guy lay there for a moment, breathing heavily. Then his body started to shake. Alarm bells began to ring in Tom's head. Was he all right? Had she hurt him? Was he having an allergic reaction to the medication?

She looked over at Ben, who was already heading in her direction. When she returned her attention back to Jacko it was to find him rolled over onto his back, his lips tight in a grin as his body continued to shake with laughter.

'Is he all right?' she asked Ben the instant he was by her side.

'He's fine.' He plonked the Santa hat back on her head. 'He's just relieved, that's all. Aren't ya, mate? The build-up and the tension of the whole thing is always the worst part.'

'Oh, Dr Tom.' Jacko slowly got to his feet. 'That was amazing. You're amazing.' He stabbed a finger in her direction. 'I want her treating me from now on.'

'You've got it,' Ben said. Jacko held out his hand to Tom.

'No hard feelings. I hope I didn't hurt ya.'

'I hope I didn't hurt *you*.'

'Ha. Funny, too. Nah. I'm just fine.' And with that he hefted her into his arms and placed her up on his shoulders, carrying her all the way around the perimeter of the yard just like football stars did after a successful game. Everyone cheered and clapped and Tom had never felt anything like it in her life. After she'd been returned to Ben's side and received the congratulations of many a person, including James and Matty, Tom began to feel the after-affects of her tussle. The tea-bell rang and the crowd dispersed, heading over to the tucker-shed, only Ben and herself left.

'Whew!' She leaned against the rails and stabbed a finger into Ben's chest. 'That was fun.'

'And you won fifty bucks.' He held the money out to her.

'You were betting on me?'

'Sure. Everyone was. We're Aussies. We'd bet on two flies crawling up a wall, but I knew you'd win, especially when you went into those flips. Highly impressive, Thomasena. Highly impressive.' And so was the way he was looking at her. Her stomach started doing flips of its own and her heart rate began to increase.

She needed to look away, to do something, to concentrate on something else—*anything* else except the way Ben was making her feel. Tom frowned as she looked down at her trousers. 'Well, these are completely ruined.' She made a vain attempt to brush the dirt out. There was a loud rumble above them and they both looked up.

'Don't worry about it. If you stand outside any longer, the rain will get them clean.'

'Rain? What rain?'

And then the heavens opened, drenching the two of them within an instant. Tom stared at Ben, her body absorbing the shock of being suddenly wet through. Laughing, Ben couldn't help leaning over and placing a quick friendly kiss on her cheek.

That rain.' Then he slung an arm about her shoulders and led her towards the homestead.

CHAPTER FIVE

AFTER she'd changed her clothes and headed over to the tucker-shed—as it was called—she walked into the large dining area and was greeted with another round of applause. It was an amazing feeling and, for the first time in her life, she began to feel as though she was accepted for who she herself was rather than whose daughter or whose wife she was.

She was now a fully fledged member of the outback. She saw respect in a lot of the men's eyes and this time, instead of trying to flirt with her, they treated her like one of the locals. Ben and Matty sat opposite her at the table and James was by her side.

'You were awesome, Mum.'

Her eyes misted at his words. 'Thank you, darling.' He was looking at her with respect and it was an amazing feeling, fuelling her new-found confidence. She breathed in, making the tears disappear before she made a fool of herself and people noticed.

Ben placed his hand over hers and she looked up at him. 'You all right?' he asked softly, and she realised he'd witnessed her emotions.

'I'm fine.' She smiled her reassurance, hoping he'd

remove his hand because the heat from his touch was beginning to travel up her arm, warming her body through and through. She was still trying to recover from the kiss on the cheek he'd surprised her with just before they'd headed inside to get out of the rain. For a man who professed he wanted to keep their relationship strictly professional and platonic, he was doing a poor job.

Tom guessed some might have called the peck on the cheek nothing more than friendly but it was too much for her and the more Ben persisted with this touchy-feely friendship, the more she was in danger of wanting more.

Then again, she didn't want to make too much out of too little. Perhaps Ben was the type of man who made a habit of giving quick, friendly kisses to the women he knew. She hoped that didn't mean he was like her husband. She'd been married to Walter Bates for a whole decade and yet after his death she'd realised she'd never even known him. In fact, she probably knew more about Benjamin than Walter—and she'd only known Ben for twenty-four hours.

Thankfully, he removed his hand and leaned back in his chair. 'Relax, Tom. Don't overthink things—simply enjoy.'

What was that supposed to mean? she wondered. She was about to ask him but thought better of it. Perhaps he was referring to the tension that existed between them. Was that what he was planning to do? To not overthink it and let the wind blow them where it may? Tom wasn't at all sure she could do that.

After the meal she returned to the living room where they'd held their clinic and began to pack things up. Ben had told her they would leave as soon as the rain had stopped but as she was packing up the last of their medical supplies, he came over and sat down in a comfortable sofa chair. 'Change of plans.'

'Oh?'

'You're going to have to forgo your first taste of sleeping under the stars in the outback.'

Tom shuddered. 'Is that what we were going to do? I thought we were camping. Like in a tent.'

'Er...no.' His grin was his answer. 'Besides, I reckon you would have loved it, Tom.' At least, he had hoped that she would. For some reason he was determined to show her the different flavours of outback life. He wanted her to see everything. Whether it was to push her away—to force some distance between them—or to help her to find the beauty in the untamed landscape so she'd never want to leave it, he wasn't sure. One hand didn't seem to know what the other hand was doing and he wasn't a man who liked conflict within himself. 'Anyway, the place we were headed—Acid Property creek—'

'What is it called?'

'Acid Property. I know. There are some strange names out here.'

'You wanted us to camp at a place called Acid Property?'

'It's very beautiful, despite the name. The point, Tom, is that Dave said that some of his men were down that way this morning and there were croc tracks in the area.'

'Crocodiles?' Alarm bells began to ring inside her head.

'Yes. So it's not safe to camp there, especially if the creek is as swollen as Dave said it was.'

'Well. Good.' The tension eased out of her as quickly as it had come. 'So what do we do instead? Head back into town?'

'Nope. Dave can put us up for the night. You and Matty will be sleeping in the house in the spare room but Jimmy and I can sleep out in the bunkhouse with the men.'

'Why can't Jimmy sleep in the house, as well?'

'Not enough room. Two other families are staying over,

as well.' He shrugged. 'There's a bunk-bed spare in the bunkhouse so we'll be fine.'

'No. James can sleep on the floor by my bed. Or I'll sleep on the floor and he can take the bed. I don't want anything to happen to him.' Because if it did, if something happened to her son, she'd never forgive herself for bringing him out here. He was old enough, she knew that. Old enough to understand the dangers and to learn what to do but he was also vitally important to her. He was her son. The one person she could count on, rely on, and she needed to protect him at all costs. Thinking of him sleeping out in the large building with all those men—men she didn't know—was causing her anxiety.

Ben stood and walked over, placing a hand on her shoulders, seeing her obvious agitation. 'Remember earlier when you said you weren't sure how to deal with a teenage boy?'

She tried hard to ignore the feel of his hand, the way it was bringing those now familiar tingles of excitement. 'Yes, but that has nothing to do with anything. James is my son. I'm responsible for his well-being.'

'No one's denying that, Tom. I'm responsible for Matty.'

'But she'll be staying in the house. There could be anything out in those bunkhouses. Spiders, for example.'

'I wouldn't say that too loud if you don't want the cleaning staff to hear. They take their jobs very seriously. Jimmy will be fine out there. For you to insist he stay inside with the women—well, it won't do his confidence any good. It's a guy thing. Trust me on this. Besides, *I* have the problem of convincing Matty to sleep in the house.'

'Why? If it's good enough for James to stay in the bunkhouse, why isn't it good enough for Matty?'

Ben dropped his hand and raked it through his hair, revealing his frustration and confusion where the fairer sex was concerned. 'Because, despite the lengths she goes to to fit in, to be the tomboy she loves being, she's also still a girl and one who is developing faster than her father is comfortable with.'

Tom nodded. 'Good point.'

'We'll swap for the night. You have Matty, I'll have Jimmy. I promise I'll take good care of him just as I know you'll take care of Mat. Jimmy'll be fine and it'll be good for him. Lots of testosterone.'

'Hmm.' Tom wasn't happy about the arrangements but conceded he had a point. She knew James would like it. She also knew he was getting older and into territory that was totally uncharted for her. He needed a good strong male influence. The question was, was Ben good enough? She wanted him to be but she wasn't sure why. 'Do you want me to talk to Matty? Explain why she needs to sleep inside?'

He looked relieved. 'Would you?'

'Sure. Why don't you go break the good news to James?' She sighed.

'It would be better if it came from you.'

'Why?'

'Because then he'll see that you're giving him the chance to try something new, that you trust him, that you're starting to loosen that umbilical cord.' He grinned as he spoke and succeeded in making her smile. It warmed his heart.

As predicted, James was thrilled when Tom explained the sleeping arrangements and went off with Ben to get their overnight bags and settle into the bunkhouse.

'It's not fair,' Matty grumbled as she flopped down onto the bed next to Tom's.

'It's completely fair,' Tom replied, sitting crossed-legged on her bed, brushing her long black hair. 'Like it or not, Matty, you're growing into a woman.'

'But I can do anything a boy can do.'

'There's no disputing that.'

'So why can't I sleep out in the bunkhouse?'

Tom stopped brushing and looked earnestly at the girl. 'Because you're growing into a woman.' She said the words with emphasis. 'Like it or not, men look at us as fragile little creatures who need protecting. It's the way they're genetically designed.'

'It's chauvinistic.'

'Perhaps, but we have an even greater weapon.'

'We do?' Matty leaned up on her elbow, her interest captured. 'What's that?'

'Feminine…power.'

'Sounds amazing.'

'It is.'

'How does it work?'

Tom felt excitement bubble through her at having a girly conversation, unable to remember the last time she'd had one. 'Well, men, due to their inbuilt need to protect, underestimate us. *That* is our power.'

A dawning realisation came into the preteen's eyes. 'Like Jacko today. Everyone—and I mean *everyone*— thought you wouldn't be able to do it.'

'Except your dad. He had confidence in me.'

'But you took Jacko's chauvinism and turned it on its head.' She clapped with delight.

Tom straightened her shoulders and grinned, once more feeling as though the shackles of her past were falling off. 'I did, didn't I?'

'So tell me how I can use it.'

'All right, but there are also some rules that go along with it.' Tom slipped beneath the cool cotton sheet and switched off the light, the open window providing a bit of moonlight, the ceiling fan whirring gently as she opened Matty's eyes to a world the girl had never known before.

Even though she'd stayed up for a few hours chatting with Matty, Tom didn't sleep well and she knew it was because she was concerned about James. She kept telling herself he was a big boy now—literally, as well as figuratively—and she needed to start letting go…to a degree.

When there was a soft knock on the bedroom door, she was instantly awake. 'Tom? Tom?' The door opened and Dave came in, his face as white as a ghost's.

'I'm awake. What's wrong?'

'It's Shelley.' The unflappable farmer was in a complete dither. 'She went to the toilet and slipped. She fell down. She's still lying on the floor and she said she has bad pains.'

'I'll be right there. Go wake Ben.' Tom dressed quickly and headed up the hallway of the long homestead towards the master bedroom. She didn't need to guess which one it was as she could hear Shelley groaning and panting. The light was on and Tom rushed to the woman's side, pressing her fingers to Shelley's neck, feeling for a pulse. 'Rather fast. What happened?'

'I slipped. It was stupid but I hit my stomach on the floor and the baby's stopped kicking. He kicks all the time and now he's stopped.' Her eyes were wide with fear.

'Right. Let's shift you onto your left side.' They managed to do that and Tom pressed her fingers to Shelley's abdomen, feeling for the contractions. 'There's one.' She looked at the clock and started to time them, waiting for the next one. She'd forgotten to tell Dave to bring a medical kit and hoped Ben would pick one up on his way. While she waited, she found a glass and filled it with water. 'Is this water all right to drink?'

'Yes. It's rainwater.'

'I guess you'd have plenty of that at the moment. Just sip it.'

'What's going to happen? I'm so worried. The others were both fine pregnancies. I didn't have any problems and was able to leave here about a month before I was due, travel to Darwin and stay at a friend's place until I went into labour. Why? Why did I slip?' Tears rolled down her cheeks.

'Shh. It's going to be all right. We're going to do everything we can to look after you. Did you have any cramping before you fell?'

'No.'

'And now?'

'Yes. Lower down, though.'

'That would be the cervix contracting. What about higher up? Menstrual-like cramps?'

'Yes, but they're not too strong.'

'Good. Back pain?'

'Yes. Lots of back pain.'

'Shelley?' Dave rushed back into the room, Ben right behind him with a medical kit in his hands.

'Marvellous. Here's the cavalry.' Tom waited for Ben to put the kit down and immediately pulled on a pair of gloves. 'Dave, go behind Shelley and support her. Rub her lower back gently. Ben, do the vitals. I'll do an internal. Shelley, I need you to lie on your back for a moment. Sorry about this.'

With her husband there, Shelley was calming down. 'No need to apologise. I've had two before.' When the next contraction came, Tom checked the clock.

'Contractions ten minutes apart,' she said, and Ben nodded as he pulled out the portable sphygmomanometer and wound the cuff around Shelley's arm.

'Poor thing. You're being poked and prodded from all angles.' He smiled at her before hooking the stethoscope into his ears. 'Blood pressure is elevated,' he announced, before listening to her heart.

'There's vaginal discharge and she's at least two centimetres dilated,' Tom reported. 'We're going to need to get you to hospital, Shelley.'

'But…but it's too early.'

'I know.' She took off the gloves and placed her hand over the other woman's. 'I know.' Her tone was strong. 'We can, however, help stall the labour for now, possibly even stop it, but if the pain continues to be strong and persistent, you may well deliver within the next twenty-four hours. Hopefully, that won't happen but complete bed rest is a must from now on.'

'Get me my phone. It's by the bed.' Dave was not willing to leave his wife's side. 'I'll get the chopper organised.'

'Good.' Ben handed it over.

'Check the foetal heart rate,' Tom ordered, and Ben picked up the other piece of equipment he'd brought in and set it up, holding it to Shelley's abdomen. Shelley breathed a sigh of relief when she heard the lub-dubs of her baby's heart.

'He's all right. He's still there. He's all right. Oh, thank God.'

'Ben, you get the IV line in, I'll keep monitoring her vitals. Do you have a terbutaline inhaler in there?'

'Yes.' He pulled one out, took it out of its box and ripped off the plastic packaging. 'Here you go. Shelley, I'm going to set up an intravenous line. We'll need to keep your fluids up and we'll also need to give the baby some steroid injections. If you're going to deliver sooner rather than later, we want his lungs to be the best we can get them. That will help any respiratory problems after birth.' He began gathering up the equipment he would need, opening a bag of tubing.

Dave was on the phone, waking everyone up and barking orders left, right and centre.

'Dad? Tom? What's going on?' Matty asked sleepily from the doorway.

'Shelley's had a bit of a fall. Why don't you go check on her kids for me? Make sure they're still sleeping,' he instructed, and Matty headed off.

'Shelley, have you ever used an asthma inhaler before?'

'When I was younger. I used to get secondary asthma.'

'And you never had any problems with them? No heart palpitations, headaches, nausea, tremors?'

'No. No.'

'Good. Right. I want you to inhale this.' She held out the terbutaline, wanting it to work as soon as possible. When Dave had finished on the phone, Ben took it from him.

'Tom, come finish this while I call Darwin hospital and let them know what's going on.' She did as he asked, both of them monitoring mother and baby until things started to settle.

'The last contractions were fifteen minutes apart.' Tom breathed a sigh of relief.

'Blood pressure is still up,' Ben commented.

'To be expected.'

'Can I move now?'

'No. Just lie still. If we move you too early, we may risk labour starting up again. Just relax. How's the back pain?'

'Better.'

They continued to monitor her for another hour and when both Ben and Tom were satisfied, they agreed she could be transferred. There was only room in the chopper for four people and that included the pilot.

'You go,' Tom said to Ben. 'You know the protocols better than I do.'

He nodded. 'We shouldn't be too long. Be back in time for breakfast.'

She smiled encouragingly. 'See you then.'

He started to walk off then stopped, a look of worry on his face. 'I forgot about Jimmy.'

'I'm sure he'll be fine. Once he's asleep, he's out for the count. Thanks for looking after him, though. It helped.'

Ben nodded again and smiled, making Tom feel as though everything was going to be all right. Then he turned and headed out to the chopper. Tom lowered her head as the powerful machine lifted off, blasting dirt all around her. She sighed. One thing she *didn't* like about the outback was the feeling of never being completely clean. However, if that was the only thing she had to complain about, she was sure she would learn to put up with it.

With a skip in her step she headed back to her room, checking on Shelley's children herself, pleased to find them still sleeping. Matty, however, was wide-awake and was more than happy to continue chatting with her until the sun peeked over the horizon and heat flooded the new day.

By the time they were ready to go to the tucker-shed for breakfast, Tom found she couldn't stop yawning. When she saw James there, sitting next to Jacko and laughing, she smiled.

'Hey, Mum!' He stood up, walked over and in front of everyone put his arms about her and hugged her close. He'd stopped her several years ago from hugging or kissing him in public—especially at school. Now he was voluntarily showing her affection in front of all these men. Her son was growing up, and she didn't mean his height. 'You look tired.'

'I am tired. You've certainly woken up on the right side of the bed.'

'Sure did. It was brilliant, Mum. Super fun.'

She put her arm around his waist. 'I'm glad, darling.'

'Ben wasn't around when I woke up but Jacko told me there was an emergency during the night.'

'Yes. Shelley went into premature labour.' She glanced around the room. 'I thought Ben might have been back by now.'

'No sign of him yet.'

Tom frowned, hoping everything was all right at Darwin hospital. Had Shelley's labour progressed during the helicopter ride? Had Ben been forced to delivery a premature baby? She wished she'd been able to go with him to support him, but then she reminded herself that he was a doctor who was used to carrying the health of this outback community on his shoulders. Still, she was here to help. That was her job and she was starting to feel exactly the opposite—helpless.

Her thoughts continued to churn, different scenarios popping into her mind as she tried to figure out what was delaying Ben. She checked her watch and agreed with her earlier assessment that he should have returned quite some time ago. Perhaps the helicopter had run into difficulties and been forced to put down somewhere…somewhere even more remote than here. She'd read about things like that happening out here. Or, heaven forbid, something worse had happened to the helicopter.

Fear gripped her heart at the thought of Ben being in a helicopter crash and for a second she felt as though her chest was going to explode from the pressure. No. She wiped the thought from her mind, forcing herself to breathe easily. If there had been an accident, someone on this large station would have received word. No. He was more than likely delayed because he'd had to fill in a mound of paperwork. Yes. Tom breathed a sigh of relief. That was all. Ben was fine. He'd just been delayed.

Again she checked her watch and again she forced herself to calm down and relax. She didn't even want to begin questioning herself as to why she was so concerned about Ben's welfare. Sure she liked him. Everyone liked him. He was a kind-hearted, amiable man.

Whom she was highly attracted to.

She pushed the thought from her mind and turned to face her son as they walked over to where they'd sat yesterday in the tucker-shed. 'Oh, James, I've been meaning to ask. Did you and Matty do the decorations in here? It's looking very festive.' She greeted people as she spoke, waving hello to others over the other side of the room who called her name.

'Yes, we did. We've only been here a few days and already I'm sick and tired of hanging decorations. Thought it was supposed to be fun.'

'Well, it certainly brings joy and the Christmas spirit to everyone else.' She kissed his cheek and was again surprised when he didn't pull away. 'You're doing a good job, James. I'm liking the way the outback looks on you.'

'I'm liking it, too. Ben and I had a big talk last night. It was good.'

'Really?' She smiled, pleased at the way he was taking to her new colleague. 'Anything you'd care to share?'

James shrugged. 'He said it was OK to show I appreciated you. That mums like it when their sons let them hug and kiss them.'

Tom leaned over and placed another kiss on his cheek. 'It's true, but I promise not to do it too often in public.'

'Cool.'

Jacko came over and sat down where Ben had sat the

day before. Tom tried to stop herself from checking her watch every five minutes and glancing at the door in between. Where was he? Why was he taking so long?

Jacko kept them all amused during breakfast with stories about outback legends, as well as throwing in some yarns of his own. Even when they'd finished eating, there was still no sign of Ben and Tom's anxiousness had increased. She was about to go and ask someone if she could use the phone to call Darwin hospital and get an update when she heard someone call her name.

'Hey, Doc!' She turned to see Jacko slouching against the doorjamb. 'Look what I found.' He pointed upwards to the mistletoe hanging above him. 'Come on, Doc. It's only fair,' he joked, and a few of the men started laughing. 'Gotta thank you for stickin' it to me yesterday.'

Tom turned wide eyes to Matty and James, who were sitting next to her. 'Will you stop hanging that infernal stuff above every door? What am I supposed to do now?'

Both kids joined in the laughter. 'It would be impolite to refuse such a...' James searched for the right word.

'Romantic offer,' Matty supplied for him, and both went off into peals of laughter again.

'I'm waiting, Doc,' Jacko continued, puckering up.

'Don't worry,' came a deep voice from behind her, and she turned to see Ben standing there.

'You're here.' Relief flooded through her. 'I was getting worried.'

'Really?' He seemed surprised but touched by her concern.

'Do-oc,' Jacko said in a sing-song voice.

Ben looked away from Tom over to the big oaf near the door then grinned at her. 'That mistletoe getting you in trouble again?'

'Yes.'

'No sweat. I'll take care of this one.' He patted Tom on the shoulder then walked over to Jacko, standing in the doorway beside him. Opening his arms as though he was going to embrace the large man, Ben said, 'Well, here I am. Your doctor. Can't say you're really my type, Jacko but—'

Raucous laughter cut off anything else Ben was saying and even Tom managed to laugh. Jacko pushed Ben away good-naturedly.

'I didn't mean you, ya drongo.' Jacko laughed before he walked off, shaking his head, leaving Ben standing in the doorway by himself. Tom's admiration for Ben increased. He really knew how to handle these wild Aussie blokes— well, he *was* one but, still, he handled them without being mean, without malice and without losing face. He'd shown himself to be honourable and true, honest in all his words and actions since they'd met. Had she found a man who was, indeed, trustworthy? Hope started to grow within her. Ben had told her to relax and not overthink things so she decided that from today onwards she was going to try and do just that.

She wasn't one to act impulsively, had always preferred to sit back and watch what happened first before venturing into any new territory. No. That was what *Thomasena* would do. As a daughter and a wife, she had always let others lead. Not this time. Since coming to the outback she'd begun to realise that she could be anyone she wanted—especially if that meant she could be the person deep down inside who had been repressed for too many years. Running on pure instinct, something she hardly ever did, Tom walked over to Ben.

'Thank you,' she said.

He shrugged as though it was nothing. She looked in-credible that morning in a light pink T-shirt and a pair of three-quarter, lightweight denim jeans, a comfortable pair of running shoes on her feet. Her scent was fresh and bright and he knew he was fast becoming addicted not only to it but to her. Things couldn't have moved more slowly at the hospital and he'd been impatient to get back so he could see her again. It was dangerous, he knew, but he hadn't been able to get his mind off her.

Now she was here. Standing before him. A vision of loveliness. How on earth was he going to be strong enough to keep his distance? The impulsive kiss he'd placed on her cheek yesterday had only made matters worse and he knew that soon he'd be done fighting the growing attraction he felt for her.

Tom watched as his hypnotic brown eyes seemed to devour her. 'You'd better be careful, Tom.' His voice was deep and husky and filled with desire. He pointed up to the mistletoe, as though giving her fair warning of his waning self-control.

She didn't even bother looking up. 'Why do you think I came over?' she whispered, before stepping closer, putting one arm around his neck and drawing his head down so their lips could finally meet.

CHAPTER SIX

BEN WAS STUNNED, to say the least, but that was no reason
to stop what she was doing, especially when it was what
he wanted her to be doing. She leaned into him so he was
against the doorjamb, one hand still around his neck, the
other resting lightly on his chest.

When she opened her mouth, he accepted what she offered and kissed her back. Surprise still existed between
them but that only made them both hold back, giving just a
tiny piece of themselves to this sudden but welcome contact.

Ben began to get over his shock and rested his hands
lightly at her waist but, in the next instant she pulled
back, looking into his rich deep eyes, seeing the passion
flaring brightly.

'Wow! Way to go, Doc.' A bloke slapped Ben on the
shoulder as he walked by. It was then Ben and Tom became
aware of the noise around them. There was clapping, cheer-
ing and a few wolf whistles.

'They sure are a noisy bunch,' Tom said, trying to cover
her embarrassment. She glanced over to where Matty and
James were standing and while Ben's daughter was joining
in the noise, James was quite the opposite. His face was
devoid of emotion, his hands clenched at his sides.

'James.' Her tone was pleading and she began to walk towards him, but he merely turned and ran from the room. Ben put a hand on her shoulder.

'I'll go.'

'No.' She stopped him. 'It's my fault. I need to fix it.'

'It's not your fault.' Ben kept pace with her as she headed out.

'It is.'

'It's mistletoe, Tom. It's a funny, silly, Christmas tradition.'

She stopped and whirled around, pinning him with a hard look. 'Meaning what?'

'That the kiss doesn't necessarily need to mean anything.' He shrugged. 'It's just…Christmas.'

'Thank you. Thank you very much.' She continued on her way.

Ben pushed an impatient hand through his hair. 'I didn't mean it like that. It came out wrong.'

'You've got that right.'

'Tom. Wait.' He took her arm but she pulled it free and continued on her way.

'No. I need to find my son.' She saw James ahead of her, going into the bunkhouse he'd slept in last night. What had she done? And he'd been so happy that morning! 'James?' she called, knocking on the door before opening it, hoping no one else was in there, getting changed. Well, if they were, they'd have to deal with it. She was a doctor after all. It wasn't as though she hadn't seen a naked human body before. 'James?' Tom put her head around the door and checked the coast was clear. 'Darling?'

'Don't.' He was sitting on the bottom bunk, back against the wall, his head touching the bunk-bed on top. He was getting so tall and she saw then that he wasn't her little boy anymore.

'James. Let me explain.'

'You don't need to say anything, Mum. You kissed him.'

'It was Christmas. Mistletoe.' She was desperate for him to realise that kissing Ben didn't mean she was trying to find him a father or a husband for herself. The only man he'd ever seen her kissing had been Walter so it must have been jarring for him to see her with another man— even if it was only beneath the mistletoe. 'It's just a bit of fun.'

'I told Matty to stop hanging it over the doorways but she wouldn't. She *wouldn't*, and now she's gone and ruined everything.'

'Ruined what?' Tom sat down on the bed beside him, and as he used to when he was little, he shifted over, not wanting to touch any part of her. 'Talk to me, James. Please?'

'You said we were coming out here for a new start. You said things would be different.'

'And they are.' She paused, searching for the right words. 'James, the last few years have been very difficult—for both of us. I know that.'

'That doesn't mean you get to go and kiss Ben.'

'Did you want me to kiss Jacko instead?'

'Sure, but not *Ben.*'

Her eyes widened at that. 'I thought you might have been upset because I was kissing someone who wasn't your father. You've never seen me with anyone but your dad.'

'What? He was awful to you, Mum. I didn't even think of that. It's Ben, Mum. Ben is *my* new friend, too. He's funny and he knows stuff. He told me last night that I was doing a good job of looking after you. That he was proud of me.' James clutched his hand to his chest. 'It made me feel grown-up. It made me feel like a man, Mum, and today you've gone and ruined it.'

'Wait. Let me get this straight. You're upset because I kissed a man you hold in high esteem.'

'Yes…whatever that means. Ben makes me feel good about myself. No other grown-up man has ever done that. Not Dad, not Granddad, not any of my teachers. Ben listens when I talk. He laughs when I make a joke. He treats me like a person.'

James couldn't know how painful his words were to hear and Tom fought back the tears. 'That's good, darling.' Wasn't that what she'd been after? A strong male influence for her son? 'I'm glad he makes you feel that way.'

'It doesn't matter. He likes you better.' James went down, burying his face in the pillow. 'He likes you better.'

'That's not the case,' Ben said from the doorway, and both of them looked up. How long had he been standing there? How much had he heard? 'Jimmy, it's not a matter of liking you better than your mum, or vice versa. You're two different people. I like you both differently. Your mum's a great doctor and I've just been trying to help her settle into the rather unique ways we sometimes practise medicine in the outback.'

'And that includes kissing her?' James asked, the pain in his voice quite clear to both adults.

Tom wasn't at all sure what Ben would say to that. Was he going to promise not to kiss her again? To keep his distance? She hoped not yet at the same time she couldn't bear to have her son hurting.

Ben grinned at them both. 'Why? You want me to kiss you, instead?'

It was the most perfect thing to say. Facetious, but perfect. James smiled and shook his head. 'Er…no, thanks, but that's not what I meant.'

'I know, mate. I think your mum and I need to make a

pact, though.' He looked at Tom. 'No more kissing beneath the mistletoe—even if we happen to be standing beneath it.' It was necessary for him to say that, to put such restrictions on them because finally having his mouth pressed to hers had been so powerfully incredible, he wanted to repeat it over and over—and that wouldn't do any of them any good... Well...it would be *good*, probably better than *good*, but it wouldn't help the situation. Hopefully, by abstaining, the cravings to hold her against him and plunder her sweet and luscious mouth to its fullest depths would decrease and he'd actually be able to sleep properly at night rather than constantly think about her.

Tom knew it was for the best and stood, squaring her shoulders. 'Agreed.' She held her hand out and they shook hands, sealing the pact, both of them ignoring the flare of longing that passed between them.

'There. All fixed, yeah?' He dropped Tom's hand as though it was a hot potato and looked at her son. James looked from one to the other, then finally nodded. 'Good. OK. We've gotta get packed up and on to the next homestead, which is about another two hours' drive.' Ben pulled out a bag from beneath the bottom bunk. 'You and Matty will be able to watch another DVD.'

'Cool.' James hoisted himself up onto the top bunk and began gathering his belongings. Tom felt like a third wheel and covered it up with a smile before heading for the door.

'Guess I'd better go do the same.'

'Yep,' was the answer she received from her son. Ben looked at her, a hint of sorrow in his eyes, but his expression said it was for the best. She nodded in unspoken agreement and went out, walking slowly up to the homestead. Matty called for her to wait and came bounding over, linking her arm through Tom's.

'So…you and my dad, eh? Dah-dum-da-dum,' she sang, stepping slowly in time to the out-of-tune wedding march.

'It was a kiss beneath the mistletoe *you* keep hanging up.' Tom forced herself to laugh. 'Nothing more.' She didn't sound convincing even to her own ears.

'You didn't look as though you were fighting it too hard.' Matty giggled. 'You even walked over there to him.' She gasped. 'You *wanted* to kiss him.'

Tom coloured at this realisation from someone so young. Had everyone seen through her impulsive decision? And now with James's reaction, was it a decision she was going to regret? She shook her head. 'Come on. We need to get packed. Ben said we're leaving soon.'

'Ben? You called him *Ben*. That's the first time I've heard that. You usually always call him *Benjamin*. I have noticed that you've been calling me *Matty* rather than the boring *Matilda* my mother insisted on. Yech!'

'Perhaps it's because I'm getting to know you better. It takes me a while to feel comfortable around strangers.'

'We're hardly strangers. Especially now that you've played sucky-face with my dad.' Matty broke off into a fit of girlish giggles once more and Tom shook her head and smiled.

'I wonder who you inherited your craziness from?'

'Oh, my dad. Definitely my dad.'

Tom paused, wanting to ask the question that was on the tip of her tongue, but wasn't sure whether she should intrude or not. She wanted to know more about Ben's past and she knew Matty would willingly supply her with some answers. 'Your mum wasn't crazy like that?'

'What? No way!'

'So you remember your mum?'

'Sure. I was six when she left, well, when she left for good. She'd usually leave and go to Darwin or Sydney or one of the capital cities for months at a time, then come home. One day she just didn't come back. Dad was really sad for a while. I didn't understand what was going on but now I do because I'm older.'

Tom smiled at the mature-sounding Matty and guessed that the age of six seemed far off to someone who was almost thirteen.

'Lin explained it all to me one day. Dad doesn't like to talk about Mum,' she said by way of explanation. 'All he's told me was that she fell in love with the romance of the outback before she even got here.'

'Your dad didn't meet her here...well, in Blaytent Springs?'

'No. They met at uni. Dad was in med school and Mum was doing some sort of English degree. Australian poems and stuff. That's why she called me Matilda. Dad said Banjo Paterson was her favourite. I've gotta admit, he's kinda cool for a dead poet guy. I'm not big into all that arty stuff. Dad says I'm more like him, that I lean more towards the sciences. Guess that's why I wanna be a vet.'

'So that's what you want to do, is it?' They headed up the steps into the house.

'Yep. Love animals. I'd love to get a few dogs and stuff but Dad says there are enough animals in the town already and, besides, Lottie lets me help out during holidays. I've seen a cow being born and a horse. Of course, I've seen kittens being born but who hasn't? I've even seen a horse having its teeth pulled. Last holidays Lottie let me file the teeth of three horses. It was way cool.'

Matty continued to talk as they packed up their belongings and said goodbye to the staff. Tom had realised she hadn't asked Ben about Shelley's condition but as he hadn't looked too grave when he'd finally arrived back, she'd presumed things were all right. She'd ask him, to be sure, though. She felt awful for neglecting her duties as a doctor but she'd been too preoccupied with other emotions. First her worry over Ben, then James.

Tom was aware of the tension in the car as they left Torch-wood homestead and headed north. The children put on a DVD and plugged in their headphones, leaving Ben and Tom sitting in silence, the car eating up the road as they drove into the heat. Finally, Ben put a CD on and this time, instead of bumpy-jumpy Christmas music, it was soft and soothing orchestral carols.

Tom searched her mind for a neutral topic of discussion. She'd had to make small talk at many a party over the years so this shouldn't be too hard. It was ridiculous to discuss the weather because all she could say was that it was hot and muggy and, besides, they'd sort of covered the strange monsoon-type weather the outback offered. Discussing their children was out, especially after this morning. No way was she going to mention the word *mistletoe* and all that had transpired around the little plastic decorations. She'd already asked about Shelley before they'd got into the car, and Ben had told her that the hospital had been able to stop the labour but that Shelley would remain there until her little one was born, which hopefully wouldn't be for another few weeks.

When he started humming along to the carols, she said, 'You have a lovely voice.'

'Er…thanks. Sorry. Didn't realise I was singing.'

'Don't apologise. It's nice.'

He laughed. 'You'd be one of the few to admit it. Usually Fitzy kicks me out of the bar when I start to sing.'

'Sure, but are you roaring drunk when you do it?'

'No. Two light beers is my maximum and has been

since I qualified. Being on duty twenty-four seven means no boozing.'

'You don't need to worry about that now. Once I'm more settled and familiar with how things are done, if you wanted to take a weekend off, please do so.'

'Thanks, but even if I did, getting roaring drunk—as you so eloquently put it—is something I haven't done since my university days.' He paused. 'Nope. Tell a lie. I got absolutely smashed when Lavinia finally left.'

'Your wife?'

'Ex-wife. Yes.'

'Matty said she was studying English when you met at university.'

'Matty spoke about her? That's surprising.'

Tom grimaced. Now he'd probably realise she'd been curious about his ex-wife. 'We talked about many things last night…and early this morning. After you left for the hospital, Matty was wide-awake.'

'No getting her back to sleep once she's awake, or it's very difficult to. I'm glad you had a good girly chat. Thank you.'

'Hey, don't thank me. I enjoyed it.'

'What did you talk about, then?'

'Aah, that's secret women's business. You would have to shave your legs and wear a dress before I'd tell you.'

'Hmm.' He pretended to consider it. 'It might actually be worth it if it gives me a clue to the inner workings of the female mind.'

'You're either insane or stupid if that's your goal in life.' She laughed, feeling happy they'd been able to get back onto an even footing.

'You're probably right,' he agreed, and changed the music to an upbeat Christmas CD. 'Now, *these* are real Christmas carols.'

Tom listened to the lyrics. 'I've never heard these before.'

'The tune's the same but the words are different. Twelve days of Christmas—Aussie style. No partridges in pear trees for us. Give me an emu up a gum tree any day.' He pointed out the window as he spoke and Tom was surprised to see an emu running in the paddock beside them.

'Will it come in front of the car?' He was travelling pretty fast and her mind raced back to the kangaroo he'd expertly avoided the previous day. Didn't these animals understand that cars meant danger?

'No. They're not as dopey as the roos. He'd give us a race, though.'

Tom watched in amused fascination as the emu ran parallel with the car for a while before turning and heading in a different direction. 'Amazing. I've never seen an emu before.'

'Not even in a zoo?'

'No, and now, in the two days since I arrived, I've seen both animals on the Australian coat of arms. The kangaroo and the emu.'

'I take it you know why those two animals were chosen?' he quizzed.

'Of course, because neither of them can walk backwards.'

'Really?' Matty said from the back of the car. 'I didn't know that.'

Ben shook his head. 'What are they teaching you at school?'

'Nothing. I don't go to school.' She laughed.

'School of the air—correspondence, via computer or otherwise—still counts as "school", Mat.' Ben smiled at her in the rear-view mirror and as their DVD had finished, Matty and James joined in the discussion so that when they arrived at the next homestead, everyone was talked out and ready to stretch their legs.

They ate lunch and then, much the same as the day before, an area was set up in the main house for Ben and Tom to see patients. Ben placed her slightly misshapen Santa hat on her head.

'Still looks good. A bit worse for having been drenched and then dried too quickly by the sun, but it does the job.' He didn't bother tying her hair back with tinsel today and it was as though they were both doing their utmost to keep their distance. They'd made a pact and they were sticking to it.

Thankfully, at this clinic, there weren't fifty burly men who required injections. Children with runny noses, babies with colic. Stomach complaints, headaches, eye tests, ear tests and three-bags-full tests. Within a few hours Tom had seen a wider variety of complaints than she would have in a whole month at the Sydney practice.

By the time the rains hit around four o'clock in the afternoon, they were done and she sat out on the veranda, watching the rain sheet down. Her feet were up on the railing that ringed the house and she was glad of the chance to rest.

'Mind if I join you?' Ben asked.

'Not at all. What are the kids doing?'

'Helping the cook in the kitchen. She's making chocolate-chip cookies.'

'No wonder James is helping. He has a sweet tooth.'

'Does his mother?'

'Not really.'

'Did your husband?'

Tom was surprised at the question but shook her head. 'No. Walter was very disciplined in his eating habits, or at least I think he was.'

'You think? That's an odd statement to make.'

'Not really.'

'You were married for what...ten years?'

'Yes.'

'Yet you don't know his eating habits?'

She sighed. 'Do we ever really know everything about the person we marry? How about your wife? Did you know everything about her?'

'No. I realise that now.'

'Hindsight. Don't we love it?'

He chuckled and looked at her, his eyes widening as he looked at her legs. 'Is that a bruise?'

'Yes. A real shiner, isn't it?'

'How did that happen?' He bent over to examine it but she shifted her legs out of his reach, not wanting him to touch her.

'I believe it occurred when I was trying to give a big brute an injection.'

'Aah. Of course. Did I tell you that you were amazing?'

'I think you mentioned something about it, yes.' Tom smiled at him, feeling the butterflies take flight in her stomach. 'But you can tell me again. I don't mind.'

Ben laughed. 'You really are quite a woman, Thomasena Bates.'

'Thank you, Benjamin.' Both were silent again as they looked out at the heavenly display before them. Lightning, thunder and a lot of rain. Tom sighed. 'It's breathtakingly beautiful.'

'It is.' He wasn't looking at the storm when he agreed.

Tom glanced at him. 'Stop it,' she warned.

'Stop what?' His voice held the same thread of desire from yesterday.

'You *know* what. We've made a pact.'

'A pact not to kiss beneath mistletoe.' He looked up. 'No mistletoe around here.'

'Ben. No. James comes first and, to be totally honest, you...confuse me.'

He nodded slowly as though he understood perfectly. 'Why is that?'

'Because for the first time in my life I'm taking care of everything. I've never really stood on my own two feet and I can't afford to fail, I can't afford the distractions.'

'You want to return to Sydney victorious. To prove to your father that you're more than capable,' he stated as though he understood.

'No. I want to get to the stage where I don't *care* what my father thinks. I want to be able to make decisions in my private life the way I do in my professional life. I want to be as certain as I can that what I'm doing both for myself and James is right, without having to question, second-guess and wonder what my father would do in a similar situation.'

'Well, I can tell you right now, your father would never have walked up and smacked a big smoochy on me this morning.'

Tom raised her eyebrows teasingly. 'Know my father that well, do you?' They both laughed but hers ended on a sigh. Silence reigned before she asked quietly, 'Tell me about your wife, Ben. Why didn't she like it out here?'

Ben stretched and linked his hands behind his head, putting his legs up on the veranda rail beside hers. 'Lavinia. Where do I begin?' He sucked in a breath and slowly exhaled. Tom remained silent, waiting patiently. 'We met at uni, as you know, and I guess you could say I was like a diamond in the rough, the typical Aussie outback bloke. I'm convinced now she fell in love with that persona, rather than who I really was. Partly my own fault, too. I was flattered a woman like her would give me the time of day.'

'A woman like her?'

'She was model material or could have been if she'd

been interested. Tall, blond hair, brown eyes. She had the voice of an angel and it was one I could listen to for hours…at first.'

Tom felt the stirrings of annoyance at hearing him speak of his ex-wife in such glowing terms. She rejected the instant claim that it was jealousy she was feeling rather than simply annoyance and listened as he continued.

'I was in my final year of med school and she was just finishing an arts degree. She loved Australian history and had the urge to see the outback. Little did she realise that the outback contained in books and poems is given a rose-coloured tinge, well, for the most part.'

'"Waltzing Matilda" is fairly descriptive,' Tom felt compelled to point out. 'Speaks of the harshness of the land, it's about a squatter—a thief, in all honesty—who, when he's caught and cornered, commits suicide in the river. That's fairly harsh.'

Ben laughed. 'I guess it is. Perhaps it was Lavinia who wore the rose-tinted glasses. After we were married and returned to Blaytent Springs, she seemed fine. Everything was quaint and very "Australiana." She wrote poems and stories. Secretly I think she had the desire to be the next Banjo. I was completing my GP training with the doctor who was working at Blaytent so I was out and about most days and sometimes not at home for a week, occasionally more. The first year was fine but when Matty was born, Lavinia began to feel trapped. She couldn't go anywhere because she had a baby to look after. She couldn't walk to the springs for a swim or, as she did once or twice, come out on house calls—like this—with me.'

He lowered his hands and shook his head sadly. 'Then she began to grow bitter. Said she was trapped and it was my fault. She wasn't able to have the opportunities in life a woman in her midtwenties was supposed to be having. She said the town was restricting her creative flow and she'd leave the area so she could work. At first it was only for a few weeks, then that changed into months, but each time when she returned she was a little more distant. Matty was about three by then so I could have her at the clinic with me on consulting days, but when it was house-call time, I had to leave her with Lottie or Lin.'

Tom nodded. 'It's far too hectic coming out here to see patients and having to worry about a small child's whereabouts and whether they're safe or not.'

'Exactly. Then one day, when Matty was about six years old, she just didn't come back. And that, as they say, was that.'

'And that's why you're determined to ensure that Matty has every available opportunity she can get?'

'I don't want her resenting the outback the way her mother did.'

'Not when you love it so much.'

Ben nodded. 'I love her so much, though. I have to say that my motives are more selfish than they appear.'

'You don't want her to resent *you?*'

Ben looked at her. 'Exactly.' He reached out and took her hand in his. 'You understand me, Tom. You understand me so well. It's as though we've known each other for a lot longer than a few days.'

'I know.' She met his gaze, saw the growing desire in there and slowly withdrew her hand. 'But where you don't want your daughter to resent you, I don't want my son to resent me, either, and this morning he did.'

Ben exhaled harshly but agreed. 'I guess that leaves us…where? Mates?'

'Mates.' Tom nodded. Both of them continued to sit

there, watching the rain. 'Ben,' she said after about five minutes, 'what was Lavinia's nickname?'

'Pardon?'

'Well, you said everyone out here gets a nickname, that it's a sign of acceptance. What was hers?'

He was silent for a moment before saying quietly, 'She didn't have one.'

'That's sad.' Tom watched the rain fall, thinking about the woman Ben had described and how her hopes and dreams had been washed away. Were *her* hopes and dreams going to end up the same way? From what she'd seen of the outback, of the slower pace of life, of the way her son was finally starting to come out of his shell, she was already half in love with it. But things could change within the blink of an eye and she wasn't as naive as Ben's wife had been.

They sat there in a companionable silence, just watching the rain, both lost in their thoughts. The rain seemed as though it would never stop, as though it could go on for ever. Tom guessed that life was like that. You woke up in the morning and you lived each day the best you could. Sometimes good things happened and sometimes bad things happened.

Each day brought something new, something different, and since Walter's death, she'd begun to realise just how fragile life could be. She'd come out here hoping to stand on her own two feet but already she'd realised this journey she was on was more than that. It was definitely one of self-discovery because if she didn't take the time to live her life now, to get to know the real Tom Bates, it might be too late.

She glanced surreptitiously at Ben and wondered where he really fitted into the equation. In such a short time he'd become important to her—that much had been evident this morning when she'd been so worried about him. Was it wrong to ignore the mounting desire between them? Was it better that they did just stay friends…at least for now?

Life was too short. She knew that. Then, just like a tap, the rain stopped.

CHAPTER SEVEN

THERE was more rain that night so they ended up staying at the homestead, which, although not as large as Torchwood, was just as comfortable. There were fewer people around so Ben and James could sleep in the house. Matty insisted on sharing a room with Tom once more.

'It appears we're swapping children yet again,' she said to Ben after dinner as they went out onto the veranda.

'Does that bother you?'

'No.'

'I know what Jimmy said this morning probably hurt you, but don't take it to heart, Tom. He's a twelve-year-old boy, with hormones out of control. He's confused, he's—'

She placed a hand on his arm. 'I know. You don't need to explain. I do understand but still…'

'It hurts?'

'Yes, but it's part of being a parent.'

'That it is. Matty seems eager for more girl time.'

Tom chuckled. 'Yes. I only hope I can actually get some sleep.' She smothered a yawn as though to prove her statement. 'Last night was a little too disjointed for my liking.'

'Not used to being called out in the wee small hours?'

'Not used to having a girl talk my ear off all night long.'

She chuckled as she recalled some of the things they'd talked about. 'She's gorgeous, Ben. You've done an amazing job with her. She's confident and well adjusted. It's nice to see someone so young know exactly what they want to do with their life.'

'Told you about becoming a vet, has she?'

'Yes. She's very keen.'

'She is.' He frowned.

'Problem?'

'I just don't want her to settle for that. She says that if she becomes a vet, she can train and take over from Lottie because by then Lottie will be more than ready to retire.'

'And?'

'Well, there are so many other professions she could choose from. Out here, though, she doesn't get the opportunities to experience anything different. What if she wanted to dance? She's a great dancer and I only wish there was a dance studio out here. I'd send her along. She can play the guitar but that's mostly self-taught and sometimes Dezza gives her some pointers because he plays.' He smacked his arm, killing a mosquito. 'I've thought about sending her to boarding school. That way, she'd be able to join a real tennis team rather than the few competitions we hold during the year. She'd be able to swim in a real pool, rather than the springs. She could take music lessons, dancing lessons, join a choir, be in a drama group, have friends her own age!'

Tom listened carefully, seeing his dilemma. 'You've made some valid points, Ben, but there's one thing boarding school will not have.'

'What's that?'

'You.'

He shook his head. 'We'd see each other.'

'You'd miss her like crazy.'

'Of course I would. She's my daughter but I've also got to do what's right for her.'

'Have you talked to her about it?'

'I've mentioned a few things here and there.'

'And what's been her response?'

'She rants and raves and gets upset. Last time she locked herself in her room and said she wasn't going to come out until I promised never to mention it again.'

'I'd say that's your answer.'

'But she's just a child. She can't see the big picture.'

'No. If you sent her away, she'd probably think that you were punishing her.'

'What? No. That's not what I meant.'

'That's how she'd take it. You're saying you want to send her away from the only life she's ever known. That you want her to leave her friends, the springs, the local tennis matches and for her to go live somewhere else— *without you.*'

'It sounds different when you say it like that.'

Tom smiled. 'Female perspective, plus the insight of a girl who was given everything money could buy, except for the one thing she wanted most—the love of her parents.'

Ben paused for a moment. 'Poor little rich girl?'

'Don't even joke about it.' Even now tears stung her eyes but she blinked them away.

'But you've uprooted Jimmy. You've taken him away from everything he's ever known and brought him into the middle of nowhere. Why is that different?'

'Because I came with him. Because we weren't happy in Sydney. Because we *wanted* something new. If you and Matty moved to Darwin together, it would be different. Would you leave Blaytent Springs, Ben?'

'Why would I leave? It's my home.' As the words came out of his mouth, so realisation dawned. He slapped another mosquito. 'Are these mozzies getting worse?'

'Yes.'

'Time to go in.'

'Yes.' Tom stood and put her hand on the screen door, stopping when Ben placed his hand on her shoulder. She looked up at him and sighed over the longing she saw reflected in his eyes. He brushed a few loose strands of hair off her cheek and tucked them behind her ear, the touch making her shiver slightly. He continued to play with her hair, letting it sift through his fingers.

She couldn't move, she was glued to the spot and the heat radiating out from his body, so close to hers, was making her heart rate increase and her mind turn to mush. As though he realised what he was doing, he dropped his hand and took a step back.

'Thanks.'

'For?' Her mind went totally blank.

Ben looked at her for a moment then shook his head. 'I can't remember. You do that to me, Tom. You have the ability to drive all rational thought and sense from my brain. Just being near you makes me forget what I'm supposed to be doing.'

She nodded, the action barely perceptible. 'You're not in this alone, Ben.'

He breathed in, filling his lungs with the scent of her, wanting to lock it up and hold it for ever. This moment. This place in time. It was as though just the two of them existed. There was no one else but them, on this veranda, talking softly, being together. 'That's good to know.' He shifted closer, wanting to be near her, but she held up her hand to stop him.

'But we're just mates, right?'

'Friends, yes.' He nodded and looked at her upheld hand. He slapped it in a high-five gesture. 'Let's go deal with our kids, mate.'

That evening was far less eventful and Tom even managed to get Matty to sleep for a good solid eight hours. It was bliss. She hadn't said anything about her discussion with Ben, deciding that unless she was asked to interfere she was leaving well enough alone. In the morning they packed up and were away quite early, heading back to Blaytent Springs.

'Christmas carols again?' Tom asked as Ben switched the music on.

'Hey, it's the only time of year most people listen to them and, besides, you've never heard Australian Christmas carols so, until you know every word, I'm gonna keep playing them over and over. They'll become so lodged in your head, when we have the singalong at the pub on Christmas Eve, you'll at least know the tunes. You can make up the odd word here and there if you really can't remember them.'

'Great. Christmas singing in the bar. A Blaytent Springs tradition?'

'Sure is. We even had a little Christmas service there, too.'

'Christmas service in the pub?'

'Well, we don't have a church and everyone's usually gathered there. Pastor Piper comes from Alice Springs every year. His mum lived here as a young girl and although she passed away two years ago, he still comes. Says it's his own Christmas tradition.'

'You mentioned that a lot of people come to town for Christmas. How many?'

He chuckled. 'Wait and see when we get back. You

may even find someone squatting in your home if you're not careful.'

Her eyes widened with disbelief. 'Really?'

'Tom, Tom, Tom.' Ben shook his head but was grinning from ear to ear. 'We're gonna have to do something about that gullible streak of yours. It's far too adorable.'

Tom glanced around at the kids in the back, wondering whether James had heard the comment, but they were both glued to their in-car entertainment, headphones on. Relaxing a little, she continued their conversation. 'So when do we start practising for the tennis tournament?'

'You want to be in it?'

'Sure. Why not?'

'Excellent. I was looking for a partner.'

'Mixed doubles?'

'Yes.'

'Don't you even want to know if I'm any good?'

'Are you as good at tennis as you are at gymnastics?'

'Probably better,' she said without vanity. 'I haven't done gymnastics for years and, believe me, I'm still feeling it.' She laughed and rubbed her leg.

'But you've continued playing tennis?'

'When I could. I usually managed to fit in a practice session with my coach every fortnight.'

'Practice session. Coach.' He raised his eyebrows. 'I'm impressed. I'll definitely claim you for my partner, then.'

'Who do you usually partner?'

'Fitzy, but trust me, you have better legs than him and no doubt look better in a little tennis skirt.'

'Hey, is this about playing a tournament or ogling your tennis partner?'

'Bit of both, I'd say.'

'Ben,' she warned, dropping her voice a little. 'We're mates. That's all.' She looked pointedly at their children.

'So? Mates can't ogle each other?'

'Did you used to ogle Fitzy?'

Ben threw back his head and laughed. 'Oh, you're fitting in just perfectly, Tom. I think the outback suits you.'

A week later, she was inclined to completely agree with Ben. Outback life did suit her and it suited her son, as well. She'd even managed a phone call to her father to let him know they were doing fine.

'When are you coming home, Thomasena? The outback is no place for a woman,' he said patronisingly. 'I know you said you were leaving the clinic permanently but I've not hired anyone else to replace you.'

'I have a commitment here until June next year, Dad.'

'And what then? You haven't thought this through. Always so impulsive.'

She gaped at that comment. 'When? When have I ever been impulsive? Between you and Walter, I wasn't *allowed* to be impulsive. The two of you managed to control most of my life. Well, not anymore. I am a mother of an almost thirteen-year-old boy and my first responsibility is to him.'

'And what sort of life are you going to give young James out there? Why, he won't even be around family for Christmas.'

'You were never home, Dad.' She shook her head, not wanting to get into the same old argument. It was all in the past. She'd made the break from her father and she intended it to be permanent. She wasn't denying him access to either James or herself. He could hop on a plane any time he liked and come and visit them, but she knew he never would. 'Look, we should let the past remain in the past. I'll call next week.'

'Don't bother.' Her father's brisk tones came down the line. 'I don't know where we went wrong with you, Thomasena. Your brothers never gave us a moment of trouble.'

She could tell he was working up to the speech where he berated, belittled and blamed her for everything. 'I have to go, Dad,' she cut in, and put the phone down before he could say another word.

She took three deep breaths, realising she was handling things better than she'd done the week before, and was pleased with her progress. Then she picked up a cushion and screamed her frustration into it.

'Tom? Are you OK?'

Quickly she lowered the cushion, seeing Ben standing just inside her front door. 'Sorry. I didn't hear you. I'm fine.'

'You're not.' He came and sat next to her on the lounge and took her hand in his.

'I am.' The warmth of his touch was welcome but she wished he hadn't. She was vulnerable at the moment. Couldn't he see that?

'Don't lie to your best friend.'

'Best friend now?' She looked at him in surprise and received one of his gorgeous yet cheeky grins as her answer.

'One of your best friends,' he clarified.

'I'm fine. I was just…talking to my father.'

'Aah. I take it it didn't go well?'

She sighed. 'It never goes well but…' She took a steadying breath in and let it out slowly. 'All better. See?'

'I do.' He let go of her hand, knowing if he didn't break the contact he'd want to hold a lot more than her hand. The past week had brought a lot of new challenges for him, and top of the list was not being caught beneath mistletoe hanging in a doorway. If he and Tom were walking into the pub together, he would stop and let her go first. It was also a cause of humour amongst their friends but it was for the best. Outback life might look good on Tom but she would leave next year because there wasn't anything to keep her glued to this place if she didn't need to be. Plus, she had Jimmy to think of. If he was worrying about opportunities for Matty, Tom must also be concerned about Jimmy. The boy deserved as much right to everything the world had to offer as other boys his age. Blaytent Springs wasn't the place to provide that.

'Did you stop by for a reason or just to make sure I wasn't burying my face in a cushion, trying not to get angry?'

'Aah…' he thought for a moment. 'The second one. No! The first choice.' He paused and frowned. 'Could you go through the options again, please?'

Tom laughed and stood, and he couldn't help but look at her legs in a gorgeous pair of red shorts. She wore a white top and the flashing Christmas-tree earrings Jimmy had bought for her. She was beautiful. So very beautiful. She was also waiting for him to speak. 'Er…I didn't know if you wanted to get in some tennis practice today. The tournament is in four days' time—Christmas Eve.'

'I know. I know. Don't stress me.'

'Stress you? You could play the match blindfolded. I don't want anyone else to see how good you are, though, and most people are in the pub at the moment, keeping cool.'

'Funny, that. Usually happens on a hot day. Is that where the kids are?'

'Yes. I think Matty's definitely snagged Jimmy for her partner after she finally convinced him to have a practice yesterday.'

'He told me she was putting the pressure on.' The two preteens had become good friends and as there were a few more kids their own age in town at the moment, they were always off in a group, doing something or other. Tom was still highly protective and usually read James the Riot Act before he went out, but she also knew he wouldn't be going far—usually to the springs after lunch to keep cool.

Both she and Ben had been busy in the clinic but thankfully they'd still managed to make time for an afternoon swim before the rains hit. She was getting used to the routines and saw how these people lived simple but full lives. They appreciated everything around them, as well as each other. It was…glorious.

There were footsteps outside and both of them turned to look as Chit rapped twice on her screen door before coming in. 'There you are. Need you both. Emergency. Get your medical bags. Chopper is being fired up.'

'What's happened?' Ben asked as they walked to the door, Tom grabbing her sunglasses, as well as her hat off the hook. Those two items had become uniform so very quickly that she now didn't even need to remind herself to put them on.

'Cattle rustlers. Out at Davies Station. I've been onto them for quite some time but never had any proof.'

'Who?' Ben opened the door to the medical clinic, heading straight for the emergency bag he kept packed, opening it quickly and checking the contents. 'Tom, get me three bags of saline. Supply storeroom.' She did as he asked, while he also fumbled around, finding other things they would need. 'Keep going,' he said to Chit. 'Who are the bad guys here?'

'Those jackaroos from up north. They've only been here about eight months but ever since they came, there's been trouble. Old man Davies called through to say one of his blokes, Stu, has been shot—so have some of his cattle. I've gotta go get Lottie informed and on the chopper. In the air in five minutes, Ben.'

'Righto.' As Chit left, the two doctors continued their work, mumbling through different scenarios as to what they might find and what they might need. At one point Tom was in the supply storeroom, trying to reach a new box of gauze pads which was stored on the top shelf, when Ben came in behind her.

'I'll get that down,' he said, his body brushing up against hers.

Both of them stilled, Ben's arm still extended in the air. Air whooshed out of Tom's lungs and she closed her eyes, trying not to memorise every contour of his firm, muscled body. When she finally worked up the courage to look at him, it was to find him staring at her mouth.

Time froze around them, neither of them wanting to move, to cause any more damage than was already being done. So close, yet so far.

'We don't have time for this.' Ben whispered the words but didn't move away. 'Tom. You smell so good.' His breathing was becoming as erratic as hers.

'So do you.'

'We don't have time for this,' he repeated, knowing if he just inched forward and dropped his arm he'd be holding her…holding her close, which was what he'd been wanting to do almost from the first moment he'd laid eyes on her.

'The kids,' Tom squeaked as he shifted his feet, his thigh brushing against hers.

'James.' Ben nodded and with superhuman effort shifted back. He went out so Tom could exit before he stepped back in to get the medical supplies they needed. They finished up in silence, both working as though there was a forcefield around the other.

As they closed up the clinic and headed over to Ben's car, Tom knew the best way to get them back onto an even keel was to talk about the medical problem at hand. 'So…gunshot wound. I hadn't expected to find that out here.'

'You'll find everything out here if you wait long enough. Nothing much surprises me anymore.' Except for the way his body had reacted to her only minutes ago. Whatever this thing was between them, it was starting to get way out of hand.

'We need to find the kids and let them know what's happened,' Tom said.

'The whole town will know by now but, yes, we'll stop at the pub.' They did this and spoke to their children.

'Keep out of the rain and, if we're not back in time for dinner, eat at the pub. Fitzy will find some food to feed you both.'

'I know the drill, Dad,' Matty said, rolling her eyes at him. Then she looked at Tom, realised her father needed more, then walked over to Ben's side and hugged him. 'I know you worry about me, Dad, and that's OK. That's what dads do. I promise I'll be good and I'll make sure Jimmy is, too. Go. Do your doctor thing. We'll be fine.'

Tom's eyes widened at Matty's words. Ben merely nodded and kissed his daughter's cheek but when he turned away, Matty winked at Tom. The girl had just 'handled' her father, using her feminine power, and it had worked. Tom shook her head with a mixture of pride and concern. She was also in awe of Matty because there was no way *she* would ever have been able to speak to *her* father in such a way. She hadn't had the guts. Or perhaps it was simply that she didn't have the support. Matty had a good friendship base, as well as a terrific father so it was natural she'd feel more secure in herself.

Shaking the thoughts away, she kissed James, embarrassing him in front of his new friends, and headed back to the car to drive the short distance to the airstrip. It was the first time she'd been back since she'd arrived and it seemed so long ago.

'It feels like I've been here forever.'

Ben smiled. 'I was just thinking that. You looked so lost, so uncomfortable when I first saw you. I thought I'd made a big mistake in hiring you.'

'Oh?'

'You were so…picture perfect. A picture-perfect princess.'

'And now? I'm almost afraid to ask.' She felt his gaze visually caress her as they walked into the shed. Bertie was getting the chopper ready for take-off so they were on their own in the hot little oven.

'Now?' Ben whistled. 'Still a picture-perfect princess but one who's more sure of who she is. It's as though you've unlocked your inner Tom.'

'I like that.'

They smiled at each other and she realised how much she enjoyed being with him. True, he'd been a regular visitor in her dreams and he was definitely her first thought when she woke up in the mornings, but the awareness that existed between them had only become stronger during the past week and she was beginning to wonder whether denying their mutual attraction was still the right thing to do.

As though Ben's thoughts were running along the same track, he reached out and touched the end of her ponytail, loving the way the dark strands looked as they sifted through his hand. When she sighed, he met her eyes.

'Tom. We need to talk.'

She nodded. 'I guessed as much.'

'I know we'd said we'd just be friends and I also know you probably aren't interested in a relationship because your contract is only for six months and you've got to think of Jimmy. I know all of that but I can't stop thinking about you.' He shifted from one foot to the other and she could almost taste his uncertainty. 'I know you're still in love with your husband and I respect that and also realise that—'

'I'm here. I'm here,' Lottie said, walking into the shed, stopping whatever Ben had been about to say. The two doctors shifted apart quickly. 'Where's Chit?'

'Thought he was with you?' Ben said.

'Nope. He told me what had happened, then disappeared.'

Tom was busy trying to control her frustration at Ben not being able to finish what he'd been saying. Still in love with her husband? Did he think she was carrying a torch for Walter? She shook her head, knowing she needed to set him straight on that point at least, because it was far from true.

'Good. Everyone's here. Let's move.' Chit hurried in one door of the building and out the other. The chopper was snug and Tom felt as though she was sitting in Ben's lap, his arm around the back of her seat. Why was it she was aware of his every move? His every breath? Had it been that bad last week when they'd been driving in the car? Had she been that conscious of him then? She couldn't recall. The problem was, she was *highly* conscious of him now, *highly* conscious of the burning need to have his mouth on hers once more. Thankfully, the need to focus her mind on medical problems was of the utmost importance so she pushed her desire for Ben aside…for now.

Bertie was able to bring the chopper down quite close to where the patient was, which meant they only had to travel into the next paddock, but a ute was there, waiting for them.

'The mongrels,' old man Davies was saying as he stood beside his employee. 'Shot the best jackaroo I've got, not to mention three of me livestock.' He grumbled on for a moment more before Lottie broke in.

'Where are the stock?'

'Over there.' Mr Davies pointed.

'Lead the way,' Lottie said, and thankfully took him with her so Ben and Tom could get on with their job without interference.

Tom knelt down beside their patient and smiled at him. 'Hi. I'm Tom,' she said, introducing herself. Ben had no need to introduce himself because everyone in the region already knew who he was.

'I know,' the man said. 'I'm Stu.'

'We're going to fix you up, Stu.' He was lying on the ground. An old shirt had been rolled up and Stu was holding it against his shoulder where the bullet had gone in.

'Best place to get shot—if you're going to get shot,' Ben commented as he pulled on a pair of gloves and opened a padded bandage. 'We're gonna patch you up and get you back to town where we'll remove the bullet and get you over to the pub in time for a drink before closing time.'

'Sounds like a plan,' Stu said with a grin.

'Beer seems to be the life force of this community,' Tom grumbled.

'She catches on fast,' Ben said, and winked at her, and she couldn't help smiling at him.

'I won't even bother to give either of you lectures on alcohol abuse because neither of you will listen.'

'We don't abuse it,' Stu interjected. 'We love and respect it. Right, Ben?'

'Absolutely, mate.'

Tom just shook her head and hooked the stethoscope into her ears, assessing the wound site when Ben removed the old shirt. She knew Ben well enough now to realise he would never let Stu drink alcohol, especially if he'd just had an anaesthetic, but the *thought* of a beer would be enough to help get Stu through the next few hours.

'How y'all doing?' Chit asked, walking over. He had a little notebook in his hand and he was scribbling in it.

'We should be able to move him soon,' Ben said. 'BP?'

Tom was unwinding the cuff. 'Decreased. I'll get the saline organised.'

'How long till you want to move him?' Chit wanted to know. 'Lottie's gonna be quite a while so I think I'll get Bertie to come on back for her later.'

'Sounds good. Uh…about another fifteen minutes?' He looked at Tom, who nodded her head in confirmation.

'Right. I'll get Bertie organised.' Chit left them to finish up.

'Yep, the bullet's still safely inside you,' Ben said after they'd taken a good look at the injury. 'No exit wound. Tom's setting up a drip to help replace the fluids you've lost and once she's got that going, we'll give you something for the pain, then into the chopper.'

'She can take her time,' Stu said, sighing as he looked at Tom. 'No offence, Doc, but you sure are something pretty to look at.'

Tom smiled. 'No offence taken.'

'Should I find some mistletoe?' Ben asked, and her eyes darted up to meet his. His voice was teasing but his expression was quite the opposite, and she was a little taken aback at his dark scowl.

'I don't think that will be necessary, Ben. Besides, I'm told mistletoe is noxious and isn't allowed to grow in the wild.'

Ben couldn't believe he was jealous. Jealous of another man making a harmless comment about Tom. But there it was. He was jealous. Jealous of the way she'd smiled at Stu, of the way she'd laughed at something Chit had said in the helicopter. Jealous of her dead husband and annoyed with the pact they'd made not to kiss each other.

He wanted to touch her, to hold her, to be with her, and as they touched down in Blaytent Springs, he was hit with a moment of clarity. Like the biggest fool on earth, he'd fallen in love with another city princess.

CHAPTER EIGHT

THEY transferred Stu back to Blaytent Springs and into the back room of the clinic, where they took an X-ray to find the exact location of the bullet. 'OK, Stu.' Tom looked down at her patient. 'I'll just let you know what's going to happen next then, once you've signed the consent form, Ben and I can proceed.'

'Do I need to do the form now?' he asked.

'Oh, yes. I need to administer an anaesthetic and we must have your consent for that. Is there anything you're allergic to?'

'Eggs.' Stu paused. 'You do mean that sort of thing, don't ya?' Tom nodded and he continued, 'Because I don't know if I'm allergic to any medicines because I've never had much need for 'em. Been healthy all me life.'

'Good to hear. Do you smoke?' As she continued to take a history, Ben was moving around the room, getting everything ready.

'So many questions,' Stu remarked a little later, growing impatient.

'Aah, don't be too hard on Tom. She's just doing her job and a fine one at that.' Ben smiled at Tom, making her feel a little self-conscious. 'In fact, you're lucky she's here.

She's qualified to give you an anaesthetic. If she weren't here, I'd have to get Lottie to do it.'

'Seriously?' Tom was surprised.

Ben nodded. 'Sure. Lottie and I have had to help each other out many a time when there's only been one doctor here.'

'You should think about making the position here permanent.'

Ben frowned a little. 'It *is* permanent.'

'Since when? It was only advertised as a six-month position.'

'Because I usually can't get anyone to come out here for longer. Six months is usually the maximum.'

'I didn't know.'

'Sorry. Would have mentioned it earlier if I'd known it was of importance.' Ben was watching her closely, a spark of hope growing in his heart. 'OK. I'm ready when you are, Tom.'

Tom finished explaining the procedure Ben would perform and, once the consent form had been finalised, she nodded to Ben. 'Go scrub.'

Once Stu was anaesthetised, Tom kept a close eye on the dials and got ready to assist Ben.

'OK. Let's get this show on the road,' he said, after removing the bandage and slathering the area with antiseptic. Tom helped him to drape Stu's shoulder and watched with interest as Ben picked up the scalpel to make his initial incision.

'I hope the bullet hasn't travelled too far since we took the X-ray.' He looked at the digital image up on the X-ray screen. 'Sometimes they can start working their way all around the body. Slippery little suckers.'

'Removed your fair share?'

'I have, more's the pity. What about you?'

'I've never worked in A and E. I'm afraid I come to you

with a lot of head knowledge but nowhere near as much practical experience as I would like.'

'Well, you've obviously administered an anaesthetic before.'

'Of course.'

'I guess you wouldn't get many gunshot wounds presenting at a private GP practice in an exclusive Sydney suburb.'

'Correct.'

'Have you thought about A and E?'

'You mean working in one?'

'Well, I wasn't alluding to tap-dancing, Tom.'

She grinned behind her mask as she held the retractor for him and readied the suction. 'And I'm such a good dancer.'

'I'd believe that.' He paused, concentrating on debriding the wound to get a better look at the area. 'So? A and E? Think it's something you'd like to try?'

'I'm not sure. I've never really thought about it before. The hours would be longer and that wouldn't be good for James.'

'True.'

'Besides, I'm enjoying my present employment opportunity, thank you.'

He glanced up. 'You are?'

'Of course. How can you doubt it?'

Ben shrugged, his hope starting to increase. Was it possible he could convince her to stay? To move to Blaytent Springs permanently? To be with him? He was going too fast, too soon. It was a mistake he'd made with his ex-wife and he had rather hoped he had learnt from his mistakes.

Tom was here until the end of June. That was a long time and a lot could happen in six months. He needed to slow down, take one step at a time. But the first thing he had to do was to finish this operation and then focus on Christmas.

With three days left until the secret Santa was due to take place, he still hadn't discovered who'd drawn Tom's name. So far, he'd swapped with five different people but with no luck. Still, he was determined.

'Suction,' he said. 'Quite a bit of arterial blood here.'

'I was just thinking that.' Tom finished suctioning the area and then checked her dials. 'Oxygen sats are fine, pulse and blood pressure both normal.'

'Good. Looks as though an artery has been nicked somewhere. Bring the light in closer.' Ben searched the wound site thoroughly, eventually finding the nick and suturing it off. 'Muscle and nerve tissue looks OK. Aah. There it is. Come here, you little menace,' he said to the bullet, and Tom chuckled.

'Usually talk to inanimate objects, do you?'

'Only when they're in my patients.' He pulled it out and dropped it into the kidney dish on the trolley beside him. 'We'll just have a quick check on everything else and if you're happy, we'll get him stitched up.'

Tom concurred with his plan and, once he'd closed in layers, she began reversing the anaesthetic as Ben put a sterile dressing over Stu's shoulder.

'Where will Stu go once he's out of the recovery stage? You hardly have a ward here.'

'He can come back to my place. I can monitor him through the night but I don't foresee any complications. Everything's been straightforward.'

'You don't think we need to transfer him to Darwin hospital for observation?'

'Nah. Stu's a man of the land. Cities make him nervous.'

'Do they make you nervous?'

'Darwin doesn't. Well, that's not entirely true. Staying there for too long makes me go quietly bananas, but otherwise it's not too bad for a day visit here and there, or if I have patients to see—which isn't all that often.'

'You make house calls to Darwin? Now, that's dedication.'

'Only when it's crucial and, besides, the doctors there are good about keeping me in the loop so, no, it's not that often I need to make a house call to Darwin. Though I'll go and visit after Shelley has the baby.'

'How do you think Old McDonald is coping, being away from his farm?'

'I think he has his priorities straight. Taking his kids to Darwin for the duration of Shelley's stay is far more important than running the station. Jacko's his overseer so there won't be any trouble.'

'I doubt anyone would give Jacko trouble,' she said on a laugh as Stu started to come out of the anaesthetic properly.

'You did,' Ben pointed out.

Tom smiled and straightened her shoulders, feeling her new confidence pulse through her. 'So I did. Well, let that be a lesson to you, Dr Caruthers.'

'Yes, ma'am.' Ben smiled brightly at her, his eyes twinkling, then quickly looked away. Could she see it in his eyes? Could she see the extent of his feelings for her? Would that be a problem? 'I'll go tell everyone at the pub that Stu's fine. You be all right here?'

'I'm fine. Would you mind also checking on my son's whereabouts, please?'

'Will do. I shall tell him that his overprotective and bossy mother needs to know where he is.'

'I'd rather be called overprotective *and* bossy if it means knowing my son is safe,' she countered, not at all put out with his teasing. That was the other thing she'd learnt very quickly—to know when Ben was pulling her leg or teasing her.

'I agree with you wholeheartedly, Dr Bates, but probably because I'm as overprotective and as bossy as you are.'

Tom laughed, enjoying herself way too much. 'We do have a lot in common, don't we?'

'We do and we make a good team.' His gaze caressed her before walking from the room, wondering what on earth had happened to his self-control. Ever since he'd realised he was in love with her, he couldn't stop staring at her, couldn't stop wanting her near, wanting her close… close against him.

Was it wrong to want her to fall in love with him? For her to be where he was? Out on the edge of a cliff, over-looking the most beautiful valley he'd ever seen? Would he ruin everything if he professed his love to Tom? As he walked across the road to the pub, he saw Jimmy and Matty sitting out on the veranda and was instantly provided with two very good reasons why he needed to be careful. He was sure Matty would be happy but he couldn't be one hundred per cent sure and while he'd become friends with Jimmy, surprised at how much the boy had changed, Ben wasn't sure he'd be ready to see his mother dating.

He would need to wait. The problem there was he'd never been a patient man when it came to affairs of the heart.

Four days later, it was time for the tennis tournament. Stu had picked up nicely and returned to his job, complaining bitterly about being forced to be on light duties. As it was now Christmas Eve, the number of people in town had quadrupled and everywhere Tom went she seemed to make new friends. It was unlike anything she'd experienced before. Everyone was so open, so giving, so happy. Of course, she'd experienced holiday cheer in the busy shop-ping centres where people would greet each other with a

'Merry Christmas' or a 'Happy Holidays' but it had always seemed so fake. The same people who had served her in June with grumbling faces and never a smile had then wished her a merry Christmas and nine times out of ten they had only been doing it because their boss had told them to.

In Blaytent Springs, she was sure if she met these same people in June, they would be just as jovial, just as nice, just as friendly. It warmed her heart far more than the heat ever could. Swatting away the flies, she walked from her house to the pub dressed in her pale pink tennis skirt and matching top. Sweatbands were around both wrists and she'd packed quite a few large bottles of water in the bag she carried. Sunscreen, sunglasses and hat had been applied and she was feeling quite the local.

Smiling to herself, she waved, seeing Ben and James sitting on the front veranda, just off to the side where it was private, outside the pub, having an earnest discussion. Ben waved back but James simply shook his head and disappeared inside.

'Something wrong?' she asked, concerned.

'No. We were just discussing men things.'

'Men things, eh? Want to give me a clue?'

'Well, you'd have to don a pair of trousers and grow a beard first. Oh, and chest hair.' His eyes dipped quickly but returned to meet her amused look. 'Actually, on second thought, we'll skip the chest hair.'

She chuckled. 'Are you going to tell me or not?'

'Not. Secret men's business.'

'Ben, he's my son. If there's something wrong, whether you think I'll understand or not, I'd like to know.'

'It's nothing to worry about.'

Tom pulled a pouting face, her eyes looking sad and forlorn, and Ben felt himself begin to capitulate. 'I'm not asking you to break a confidence,' she said. 'Just give me a clue.'

Ben tugged at the end of her ponytail sticking out from the back of her hat. 'OK. We were talking about girls.'

'Girls?' She almost exploded and Ben quickly put his hand over her mouth.

'Shh.' He looked around but quickly let her go. Being close to her, especially after realising his true feelings for her, was something he craved more and more, but they were about to play a tennis match and there were plenty of people around.

'He's twelve years old!'

'He's almost thirteen, Tom. End of January, right?'

'Yes.' She sat down in the chair. 'Girls? Already?'

'Sorry to break it to you.'

'Who is it? Is it Matty?'

'No.' Ben's smile was puzzled. 'Jimmy and Matty seem to fit together more like brother and sister than anything else.'

'Thank goodness for that.'

'Meaning?' He straightened, unsure if she was criticising his daughter.

'Oh, I don't mean anything bad by it. I love Matty, don't get me wrong. It's just that being a similar age and having their parents work together, it's easier if they're just friends—you know, if they see each other in a sibling capacity.' Or if their parents ended up getting married or something strange like that, she added silently, and tried not to sigh at the thought. Being with Ben, being able to spend time with him, the two of them together…alone, it was starting to become an obsession with her. They needed to talk—both had agreed on that on the day of Stu's accident but the past few days had been so hectic with final Christmas preparations and tennis practice, there'd hardly been an opportunity.

'You love Matty?' Ben asked.

'Sure I do. What's not to love?' A smile came to her face. 'We've had some great chats, too. About *boys.*'

'No. Don't even mention it,' Ben groaned, then thought for a moment. 'Hey, wait a minute. If you've already spoken to Matty about boys, why were you so surprised that I would be talking to Jimmy about girls?'

Tom shrugged. 'Girls mature faster than boys.'

Ben stepped back and pointed his finger at her. 'That's exactly what Matty said to me last night. Exact same shrug, exact same words.'

'She was telling you about a boy?'

'No. We were having a discussion about the possibility of her going to Darwin to a boarding school.'

Tom nodded. Matty had told her in no uncertain terms what she thought of her father's idea and although she and Ben had discussed it, it appeared he still wasn't convinced he was doing the right thing by keeping his daughter with him in Blaytent Springs.

'And how did the discussion go?'

'It was different from the others.'

'Oh? How so?'

'She didn't rant and rave and threaten never to speak to me again.'

'Well, that's good, right?'

Ben narrowed his eyes into a piercing stare. 'Tom,' he drawled slowly. 'She's talked to you about this, hasn't she?' he asked.

'Yes.'

'And what advice did you give her?'

'I told her to speak from her heart but not to do it with tantrums. To be calm and clear in her thoughts, her wants and her needs.'

'Well, she was.' Ben straightened and rubbed a hand across his face. 'It completely threw me and for the first time I actually listened to what she was saying.'

'I'm happy—for both of you. Communicating effectively with her is of paramount importance, Ben.'

'Just as it is for you and Jimmy. He obviously hasn't said anything about this girl?'

'No.'

'I've suggested he speak to you. It's not my place to tell you the details but I can advise you to take everything he says with the utmost seriousness. Don't go saying what he feels for this girl is some sort of puppy love. You and I both know it is, but to Jimmy it's very powerful and it's very real. Figuring out how to deal with girls at this age will, hopefully, stand him in good stead when he's older.'

'Oh, isn't this sort of thing covered in the manual?'

Ben chuckled. 'At least we have each other to bounce things off.'

'Yes. I trust you with James and, believe me, that's saying a lot. I don't trust *anyone* with my son.'

'Well…' Her words had left him stunned, speechless. She trusted him with her *son*. 'I er…wow. That means a lot to me, Tom. Really, it does.'

She could see the genuine belief in his eyes and for a moment neither of them moved. The pull was there—stronger and more powerful than before. Tom looked up, wishing for mistletoe.

'We could go stand in a doorway if you need the excuse.'

'Ben, you know why we can't.' She wasn't at all surprised he could read her mind. It was becoming a common trait between them. She guessed it was inevitable when they were on the same wavelength.

'Actually, I forget everything when you look at me like that. I want you, Tom.'

Her breath caught in her throat. 'Ben.' His name was a whisper from her lips. 'Don't.'

He came closer and brushed the back of his hand down her cheek, caressing her tenderly before tucking a stray lock of hair back behind her ear, her hat almost coming off in the process. Tom trembled then sighed with longing.

'I love the way that piece is just a bit too short for you to tie back. I love the way your skin feels so soft when I touch it. I love the way you sigh and your breathing increases when I'm this close to you. I want you, Tom, and that want…that *need* isn't getting less, it's increasing.'

'We can't, Ben.'

'Why not?'

'There's too much at stake. James is uncomfortable about seeing me with you, for a start. We're colleagues and if things go bad…I don't want it to get awkward. I'm here until June and the town is so small and…' She closed her eyes, trying to think rationally, trying to remember all of the reasons why they couldn't pursue the frightening natural attraction that existed between them.

'I've been there, Ben. I've been the subject of inter-office whisperings. My colleagues, my patients, the people I called my friends. I was ridiculed, laughed at behind my back, and I'm not saying things will get that bad here, but I just can't take that chance. It would hurt me, it would hurt James and…' She bit her lip, trying to hold back her tears. 'And we'd have to leave.' Tom shook her head. 'I don't want to leave here, Ben. I love it here. Blaytent Springs has been a gift from above. The people are amazing, the way of life is fantastic. I want to see it in the dry, as well as the wet. I want to understand the way you run the practice, I want to be more involved. I want to keep getting to know Matty and Lin and Lottie and Chit…and, of course, you. There's so much we don't know about each other, Ben, and I want to find out, but I need to do it slowly.'

Ben didn't back off. Instead, her words had only drawn her to him even more. 'I had no idea you'd been hurt so badly.' Was it connected with the death of her husband? She hardly ever spoke about him and neither did Jimmy. What had happened and why couldn't she trust him enough to tell him everything? 'I don't know if I can back off, though. I don't want to hurt you but I am having trouble sleeping, having difficulty concentrating on my work and how—' He broke off on a short laugh. 'How anyone expects me to play tennis beside you when you're wearing such a sexy outfit is beyond me.'

'Sexy?' No one had ever called her sexy before.

'Yes.' His eyes reflected the truth. 'Tom, I don't know how things will work out between us if we pursue these feelings. I can say for my part that I'm more than interested in forming a strong attachment to you…a permanent attachment.' He was working hard at reining himself in. If he confessed his love for her, right here, right now, she might run in the opposite direction. He couldn't have that but he could let her know that his intentions were honourable. 'With regard to Jimmy, if we decide to pursue this, I'd like to suggest we sit down with both the kids and let them know we're dating. That nothing will change—as far as Jimmy is concerned. He needs to know I'm still his friend and that I'll always be there for him. I also don't want him to think I'm replacing his father.'

'Hard to replace something that wasn't there in the first place,' she muttered.

'What?' Ben was startled at her words.

'Walter. He wasn't interested in James, except when it suited him.' She couldn't bring herself to add that it had turned out that Walter hadn't been all that interested in her, either. She hadn't known her marriage wasn't normal. After all, the only marriage she'd had to gauge hers by had been her own parents' and now that the blinders had been taken off her eyes, she knew that neither of her parents were happy in their situation but rather than divorce and cause a stir, they'd simply accepted their lot in life and would continue on that way until their lives ceased to be.

'That's why you're so important to him. He's *never* bonded with anyone the way he has with you, and I'm not just paying you a compliment. James talks about you every day. He tells me certain things you've said and, when he talks, there's a light in his eyes that has never been there before. It's a light you've turned on and I will do anything to make sure that light stays there, even if it means denying myself what I want.'

Ben opened his mouth but Lin called out to them and they turned to face her.

'Sorry to interrupt but we're about to head over to the tennis courts and get this tournament started.'

'Thanks, Lin. We're coming.' Ben turned back to Tom and said softly, 'We're by no means finished with this discussion. This is the beginning, Tom.' His words weren't harsh and that cute little grin, the one that made her melt, was twitching at his lips.

'I know.'

'Let's go play some tennis, Dr Bates.' He indicated she should proceed him.

'Good idea, Dr Caruthers.' Tom stepped off the kerb and headed towards the tennis courts. Ben went to follow but Lin stopped him, putting her hand on his arm and holding him back.

'Ben—'

'Don't give me any lectures, Lin. I know what I'm doing.' His eyes hungrily followed Tom as she walked up to her son and put her arm around his waist. 'I hope.'

'I'm not going to lecture you.'

Surprised, Ben turned to look at her. 'You're not?'

'Nope. I do, however, have a little present for you.'

'Are you my secret Santa?' he asked. 'If so, I believe you're a bit early. Christmas is tomorrow.'

Lin took a piece of paper from her pocket and held it out to him. 'I'm not *your* secret Santa but I'd be more than happy to swap with you. I believe you have Chit.'

'How do you know? It's supposed to be *secret*.' Ben threw his hands in the air but then looked at the folded piece of paper she held out, realisation hitting him. 'You want to swap? It's a deal if you have who I think you have.'

'Everything working to our mutual satisfaction because, believe me, I can give Chit a better secret Santa present than you.'

Ben took the piece of paper and carefully unfurled it. The name he'd been wanting to see, hoping to get, was written on the small scrap of paper. 'Tom.' Finally.

'Got any ideas? It may be a bit late to buy her something.'

Ben's smile was full of secret happiness. 'It's all under control and I've just realised that I have the most perfect thing for her. Perfect!'

CHAPTER NINE

THE tennis match was difficult, as well as hot but both Tom and Ben managed to beat their opponents in every match and soon it was them against Fitzy and Dezza.

'We're gonna wipe the floor with you, Docs.'

'I'd like to see you try.' Tom spun her racket in her hand, bending over and swaying from side to side as she waited for the first serve. Ben was behind her and while Fitzy was getting himself psyched, still bouncing the ball on the court, she glanced over her shoulder, intending to give her partner a wink of encouragement.

Molten lava flowed through her as she realised Ben was watching her closely—too closely—his gaze travelling over her body. When he finally looked at her, he grinned, a little sheepish but not at all sorry for being caught out. Tom couldn't believe how incredible he made her feel, to know that he desired her, that although they'd played several games already, he was still ogling her. She returned his smile.

'Fault!' umpire Chit called as the ball sailed right past both Ben and Tom. They looked up at Chit, across at Fitzy, who was frowning and checking the position of his feet, then back at each other. Ben's grin increased.

'Guess we should try and concentrate if we're going to win this tournament,' he said, coming to her side. The scent of him, the sweat combined with fresh dirt and a hint of the spicy aftershave she'd come to equate with him, surrounded her senses, and she sighed.

'If you want me to concentrate, don't stand so close to me and don't look at me the way you just were.'

'Why?'

'Because it messes with my mind. It makes me feel all…funny inside and I can't play tennis when I'm like that, now, can I?'

Ben shrugged. 'I dunno. Think I'd like to see you all like that.'

Tom laughed, never having enjoyed a tennis match as much as this, and gave him a gentle shove. 'Go back to your position…and concentrate.'

'Yes, ma'am. Anything you say…ma'am.'

'Ready?' Chit called, and this time Tom forced herself to really concentrate, even though she knew Ben was still ogling her. Her senses were so completely attuned to him. She couldn't remember when it had happened but it had and now, whenever he walked into a room or was close to her, she felt him long before she saw him.

Fitzy served the ball and Ben hit it back, eager to take his old tennis partner on and win. The match was a good one and yet playing in the heat of the day wasn't at all easy, but after an hour Ben and Tom finally got a break of service and came through, winning the tournament.

James came running over to his mother and hugged her close. 'You did it! You did it!' He released her just as quickly and threw his arms around Ben. 'You guys are great together. Wow. That's better than watching Wimbledon on TV!'

Tom laughed but was glad her son was so impressed. She was also glad James thought she and Ben were good together. Perhaps there was hope after all.

After receiving their trophy, which they agreed to display in the medical clinic for everyone to see, Tom and Ben had their photograph taken for the outback newspaper. When the rains came, no one dashed indoors but calmly continued packing everything up.

'I'll walk you home,' Ben said, as Tom picked up her sports bag.

'Thanks. I was going to take a shower but now I'm not sure I'll need one.' She opened her arms wide and lifted her face up, loving the way the cooling rain felt on her skin. 'Mmm. This feels like my idea of luxury.'

'That's how I feel when we're out at the springs. It's so natural, so unique and so relaxing.' They were almost at her house. 'We should go out tomorrow morning and enjoy a Christmas swim. What do you think?'

'As long as we don't have any emergencies or patients, I think it sounds wonderful.'

'Great. The kids'll love it, too.'

She nodded. 'It's a date.'

'It is. I'll pick you up at seven o'clock. We can swim before breakfast.'

'I'm liking this more and more.' They were close again, as they'd been earlier on the veranda. Ben swallowed and she watched the action of his Adam's apple before looking at his mouth. She sighed, wondering just how she was supposed to take things slowly when all she wanted to do was to throw her arms about his neck and hold him close.

'Mum? Hey, Mum!' James came bounding up, his hair plastered to his head, his clothes soaked through, but she knew that ten minutes after the rain stopped he'd be dry once again. Tom stepped back, wondering if James had seen them. If he had, it obviously wasn't bothering him as the smile on his face was huge. 'Are we going to the pub tonight for the carol singing?'

'We are.'

James gave a whoop of joy.

'Why?'

'Because Tijana'll be there, too.'

'Who's Tijana?'

James glanced at Ben, who nodded, then back at his mother. 'She's this girl from Alice Springs. Our birthdays are both in January, although mine is two days before hers and she was telling me all about the thirteenth birthday party she's going to have and her dad used to live here when he was little and they haven't had a Christmas here for years so they decided to come this year and, boy, am I glad she did. She's really nice, Mum. You're gonna like her.'

'I'm sure I will.'

'OK. I'll go tell her we'll be there.' And he was gone as fast as he'd come.

Tom shook her head. 'It really is starting.'

'It most certainly is.' And he wasn't just talking about her son's romance. 'I'll see you at the pub.'

Tom stood watching him as he walked off, admiring the contours of his body and wishing he'd take his shirt off. The first time she'd seen him, she'd wanted him to put it on. Now…it was quite the opposite.

After showering and dressing in a cotton Christmas dress she'd ordered online—as well as a few other purchases—Tom brushed her dark hair until it shone almost as much as the piece of green tinsel she tied around it. The action brought back memories of when Ben had tied a piece in her hair the other week and she marvelled at the difference a change of scenery could bring. Or perhaps it wasn't necessarily the scenery but the people…the genuine people.

And Ben was at the centre of it all.

'You look nice,' James said as he came out of his room dressed in a pair of shorts and a cotton short-sleeved shirt, the obligatory thongs on his feet.

She twirled, the lightweight red dress she wore flaring out and settling around her calves again. It was sleeveless and trimmed with thin green satin ribbon. She'd worn many gowns during her life yet none had made her feel more of a princess than the simple lines of the dress she now wore. 'Thank you, James. So do you.'

'I look *handsome,* not *nice.*' He shook his head, as though his mother would never get it right. 'Come on. Can we go? I think Tijana might already be there.'

'Of course.' She picked up some envelopes off the table and put them in a small carry bag as James went outside onto the veranda.

'Hey, there's Ben,' he called, and waved. Tom joined her son and watched as Ben, dressed much the same as her son, came over. The only difference was Ben was wearing boat shoes rather than flip-flops. 'He's so cool, Mum,' James said.

'You really like him, don't you, darling?'

'I do. If I had a dad like him, everything would be perfect. You should marry him, Mum.'

Tom was too stunned to reply so that when Ben stood at the bottom of the steps all she could do was to look down at him in astonishment. James was chatting with him, however, so hopefully he hadn't noticed.

'Matty's already gone over,' Ben said, and as soon as

they started walking, James took off. 'A little eager, I'd say.' Ben laughed.

'Yes.' Had her son just given her permission to date Ben? To see where this attraction might lead? She wasn't quite sure but her head was spinning with the possibility, so much so that she found it difficult to concentrate as the evening got under way and quite a few times she had to ask people to repeat themselves.

Fitzy was celebrating Christmas Eve by making different cocktails, everyone 'oohing' and 'ahhing' over his creations. 'Mocktails for the kids,' he said. 'And Chit and the doctors. Who else doesn't drink?' he asked, not wanting to leave anyone out. He was inundated with orders and soon Ben went behind the bar to help him mix and shake the concoctions.

'Here you go, Tom.' Ben carried a glass over to where she was talking to Lin.

'What's this?'

'It's called a Sydneysider.' The drink looked amazing, garnished with an apple fan in the shape of the Sydney harbour bridge.

'That's amazing, although I don't feel much like a Sydneysider any more—er, the town, not the drink,' she quickly clarified, taking a sip. 'Delicious.'

'Can I get something frothy and pink?' Lin asked.

'Ooh, me, too,' Tom said, drinking the cool juice mix contained in the mocktail.

'Coming right up.' True to his word, Ben returned, carrying three glasses. 'This one,' he said, putting it down in front of Lin, 'is called Pink Froth.' The next glass he placed in front of Lottie, who had just joined them. 'This one is called Banberry. And this one—' he placed it in front of Tom '—is called Blushing Bride.'

'Ooh.' Lottie and Lin giggled like schoolgirls and Tom knew she was, indeed, blushing.

'Look at her face,' Lin said. 'You've made her blush, Ben. Now all we need is the bride part.'

'It's under control.' Tom's eyes widened at his words as he turned and walked away. Lottie and Lin continued to tease her but Tom really wasn't sure what to do or say. She kept glancing surreptitiously at Ben as he mixed drinks for his friends. A few times he caught her staring and winked at her, making her insides warm with need.

When it was time to sing Christmas carols, she was happy to join in the cacophony the locals called singing.

'Now, aren't you glad I played you all those tunes in the car?' Ben asked from behind Tom, his breath fanning across her neck and down her arm, causing goose bumps to rise.

'I am.'

He stayed by her side for the rest of the evening and when Fitzy kicked everyone out half an hour before midnight, Tom helped Ben put a few of their friends, who had filled themselves with too much Christmas cheer, to bed.

'Whew!' They headed out into the evening air, swatting mozzies and the odd fly. 'Quite a night,' Tom said, wishing Ben would hold her hand or put his arm around her or something. Although he'd been close throughout the evening, he hadn't made any effort to touch her and she was now beginning to crave it. After his comment about the blushing-bride drink, she'd been anxious to ask him what he'd meant, but now that she had him alone—James having gone to bed an hour ago—she wasn't sure she had the courage.

'This is why Christmas only happens once a year, I'm sure of it.'

'There'll be a few hangovers to be dealt with tomorrow morning.'

'Aah, Fitzy will take care of them. He has a brilliant recipe, which looks and tastes like tar.'

Tom laughed. 'Sounds as though you speak from experience.'

'There is a reason I don't drink anymore. Two light beers. That's all there ever is.'

The backs of their hands brushed together but still he didn't make any move to touch her. It was probably just as well, although she was finding it increasingly difficult to hide her disappointment. He'd been so attentive, so caring and she had simply thought he was waiting until they were alone to make another move, but he wasn't. Had she read the signals wrong?

They were almost at the steps of her house and she knew it was now or never. Taking a deep breath, she stopped walking and turned to face him. 'Ben, I don't want this to sound presumptuous or pretentious but…that is, I thought perhaps you might have been…' She stopped, took a breath and started again. 'I'm not all that experienced when it comes to…' Tom shrugged. 'This.' She indicated the space between the two of them.

'This?' He made the same gesture and she smiled.

'Don't tease me. I…I don't want to mess this up, you know, by getting the wrong end of the stick.'

'Stick?'

'Ben.' Her tone was imploring and she touched his arm gently.

'Ooh. *This*. Right. You mean…'

'Yes.' He still made no move to close the distance, to touch her. Tom let her hand drop back to her side.

'I see.' He nodded slowly. He obviously wasn't going to make it easy for her.

'OK.' She was a grown woman. She'd been married,

she'd had a child and was raising him on her own and doing a fine job, even if she said so herself. Why was she afraid to talk of her feelings? 'I can do this.'

'Do what?'

'Talk to you.'

'Of course you can. Here, let's sit on the steps.' He waited for her to sit first but, again, he was keeping his distance. 'I'm glad you're willing to talk. That's a good sign.'

'Sign of what?'

'That you're getting there.'

'Getting where?'

'Aah…if I told you, it would spoil half of the fun.'

'Right. Um…' She untied the tinsel from her hair and fluffed her fingers through it, willing the right words to come. 'All evening long I've sort of been picking up on signals.'

'Signals,' he repeated.

'Yes. From you. Signals that you were…well, I guess wanting to move this…*thing* between us to…I don't know—the next level or something like that.'

'You really aren't good when it comes to talking about your feelings, are you?' Ben smiled and it took the sting out of his words…almost.

'Hey.' Indignation rose to the fore. 'I'm doing the best I can. You try being raised by cold, unfeeling parents and then having a marriage which was pretty much a replica of that and then open up to a man you've only known for two weeks about how he makes you feel.'

'I'm sorry. I tend to tease more when I get nervous.'

'You're nervous?'

'I am.'

'Of me?'

'Yes and no. Not nervous of *you* but definitely nervous about how you make me feel.'

'Yet you don't seem to have any problem talking about it.'

'It's the outback. As I said on your first day here, we've got no secrets in this town. If you've got a problem, you tell Fitzy or Dezza about it, they tell everyone else and it's out in the open. No more problem.'

'So I should go talk to them?'

'No!' His answer was insistent. 'Listen, Tom, you said something earlier, before the tennis match when we were on the veranda, and you've said something just now that prompts me to ask you some personal questions.'

'Like what?'

'You said that you'd been badly hurt by gossip. What gossip, Tom? Do you think you can tell me?'

'It was nothing major—well, it wasn't *about* me as such. It was about my husband.'

'Your husband?'

'Yes.' She closed her eyes not at all sure how to say this. 'You've got to understand that my marriage—I always thought—was quite solid.'

'It wasn't, though, was it?'

'No.' Tom clenched her hands together.

'Hey.' Ben couldn't believe how uptight she was. Every muscle in her body was rigid and although he'd told himself to keep his distance, just until tomorrow, he knew he couldn't. He'd asked the question. He'd caused her the anxiety she was now feeling. When she started rocking back and forth a little bit, Ben groaned and gathered her into his arms. 'Hey. It's OK. I didn't mean to hurt you.'

'You haven't. You wouldn't. You're far too…genuine for that to ever happen.'

'Genuine. I can't remember if anyone has given me that compliment before.' He paused, pulling her back a little so he could look into her eyes. 'It *was* a compliment, right?'

Tom allowed him a small smile, a very small one.

'What is it? Can you tell me?'

'Yes. I want to tell you, Ben, but…' Her tension continued to increase. 'But then it will shatter the illusions you have about me. It'll make you leave.'

'Let me tell you something.' He kissed the top of her head. 'I don't have illusions about you, Tom, and I won't leave. I'm not that shallow, if I do say so myself.' He wanted to tell her he loved her, to tell her he would always protect her, to tell her he already thought of her as *his*.

'True. You're not.'

'Come on. Rip the plaster off, Tom. Why were those people gossiping about you?'

'Because he…Walter…he cheated on me.' She sighed heavily when the words came out and relaxed against him. There. Now he would see.

Ben waited for more but it didn't come. 'How is that supposed to affect what exists between us?' He didn't want to trivialise her pain—he would never do such a thing—but he was still at a loss.

'Because I'm obviously not…good.'

'Good?'

'You know…in…' She trailed off.

'In what? Relationships?'

'Sex. I mean, I'm obviously not good at sex.'

'Aren't you?'

'Well, if I was, why did he need to go looking elsewhere?'

'Because he was an idiot.'

'You didn't even know him.'

'I don't need to. And this is why you were gossiped about? Because your dirt bag of a husband had an affair?'

'Affairs. Plural. And, yes, I was talked about, although none of this came out until after his death.'

'You didn't know?'

'How as I supposed to know? I've already told you, my marriage was normal, or so I thought, but now I've come to realise that my idea of normal was what I saw of my parents' marriage. My mother and father slept in the same room, ate their meals at the same dining table—whenever my father was home and not in surgery. They went to the same parties, attended the same functions, and that's what I thought marriage was.'

'It was all you'd ever known.'

'Yes. Then along came Walter. He was tall, he was handsome and he was very charming. He flattered me, he wined and dined me and he had Dad's blessing. He was perfect. When he proposed after our third date, I was hooked and said yes immediately.'

'You were young.'

'I was more naive than young. I was still at medical school but it was just bliss. He was happy for me to continue on with my studies, to become a doctor and eventually work in the general practice he was put in charge of after our wedding.'

'He already worked for your father?'

'Yes. I asked my father just before we left to come here whether my marriage was part of the business deal. That Walter could take over running the practice if he married me. My father didn't even try to deny it.'

'Tom.' He sifted his hands through her hair but he could tell she didn't notice. She was elsewhere, thinking about her past, about the things that had driven her from Sydney to his waiting arms.

'It was my dad's way of "taking care of me." I was a daughter, I wasn't as important as my brothers, never had been. I was settled in a suitable marriage and that was that as far as he was concerned. Walter was obviously happy to keep up the pretence. I never knew. I never knew.'

Silent tears slid down her cheeks. 'I always thought we had a solid marriage. We went to the right parties, were friends with the right people. We were honoured, esteemed, other people wanted to be us—at least, that's what Walter used to say.'

'And Jimmy?'

Tom's smile was instant and she relaxed a little. 'James was my light. Walter never really had much to do with him. He was always working but, again, I thought it was normal. It was how my father had been but, for me, James was vitally important.'

'Does he know about his father's infidelities?'

'I'm not sure. Even if he does, I don't know if he fully comprehends it. He will the older he gets but it's also the main reason why he's so fiercely protective of me. He knew his father had emotionally hurt me. Several times at night, after Walter's death, I would just lie in my bed and cry. Everyone thought I was the grieving widow, but not James. It was as though he could sense my unhappiness. He would come into my room and climb into bed and he'd cuddle me. He'd whisper over and over that he was going to protect me. That no big men were ever going to hurt me. He was only ten when Walter died, but it was as though he grew up overnight.' Tom sniffed and Ben handed her a monogrammed handkerchief. 'Thank you.' She blew her nose and took a deep, cleansing breath. 'That's why we had to come here. At first, when I applied for the job, it was to get away from my father. Then, as people started talking, as the penny started to drop, as I worked up the courage to confront my father, I realised the enormity of my mistakes. James came to me one night and said we had to go. We had to get away. Somewhere new. And he was right. When I received your e-mail, saying I'd been successful, the doubts started to come. Was I doing the right thing? Plus, I had my father announcing I would fail—fail at the job, fail at motherhood.'

'No.' Ben had listened in silence, feeling frustration and anger at how she'd been treated. *His* Tom. 'You haven't failed. At anything.'

'I know that now. Blaytent Springs has been a haven for James and me. He's so happy here and so am I.'

'Are you?'

'Yes.'

'And us?'

Tom sighed. 'I'm not sure, Ben. I'm obviously a liability. I mean, if Walter didn't desire me—'

'You're insane,' he interrupted. 'Do you have any idea just how difficult it is for me to keep my hands off you? For me to keep my distance? I was starting to *look* for doorways with mistletoe just so I could have an excuse to kiss you, to hold you. Then we made that ridiculous pact.'

'It wasn't ridiculous.'

'Not the reason for it—that's as important as ever—but there has to be another way, Tom. I can't stop wanting you. I can't stop needing to hold you. You are so incredibly beautiful.'

'But that's just physical. What happens when you don't want me anymore? I'll have to leave. This is your home, Ben, and I want it to be my home, too. If things go badly between us...' She hiccuped, holding back her tears. 'It just won't work.'

'I completely disagree with you. I'll never stop wanting you, lady.'

'But tonight. You were always there, always near me, but you didn't touch me. You didn't want me.'

'Is that what you thought?'

'Is that wrong?'

'Yeah, it's wrong.' His tone was filled with utter disbelief. 'So totally wrong. I didn't touch you, Tom, because we were in a public place and I knew that once I started touching you, I wouldn't be able to stop—and did I mention we were in a public place?' His arms tightened protectively around her.

'But when we left…when we walked over here…'

'I was thinking, that's all.'

'About what?'

'My secret Santa.'

'You were thinking about…' She stopped and edged out of his embrace. 'Here I was, tying myself up in knots, and you were worried about your secret Santa?'

'Hey, it's an important part of our Christmas traditions.'

'I'm not disputing that, it's just that… Oh, never mind.' It didn't matter. Not really, or at least she told herself as much. So what if he was thinking about his secret Santa while she'd been churning and worrying? He was a guy. She was a girl. He went into his cave and she got to cry herself to sleep at night. Same planet—different worlds.

Tom stood and brushed the back of her dress. 'It's late.'

'It's Christmas.'

'It's after midnight?'

'Yes.'

'Oh.' She was a little disappointed. She'd thought this Christmas would be the best one she'd ever had but now, when the day was only a few minutes old, it already wasn't looking too good. 'I'm going to go in to get some sleep.'

Ben could see the tension on her face and although he

wanted to tell her everything, to blurt it all out right then and there, he knew he couldn't. She'd opened up to him. It was a start—a big start—because now that he knew her inner secrets, he could take a big step to helping her heal. He rose and stood looking at her for a moment. Then he took her hand in his and kissed it with such gentlemanly tenderness…just as he had on her first night there, but now the effect was greater.

'Good night, Thomasena.'

'Good night, Benjamin.'

He smiled. 'You haven't called me that in a while.'

'Ditto.'

His fingers trailed over her cheeks, his thumb brushing ever so lightly over her lips, which parted at the touch. Tom closed her eyes, willing, waiting and wanting. 'Sleep well, my Tom.'

When she opened her eyes, it was to see his dark shadow disappearing into the night. Leaving her alone.

CHAPTER TEN

'IT'S Christmas!' James was out of bed and shaking her awake the instant the sun was up, or so it seemed. Tom had managed to fall asleep around 3:00 a.m., her thoughts churning. Ben's words had floated around her and although she loved hearing him say that she was beautiful and desirable, she wasn't sure she could believe him. If she *did* believe him, it would only give him more power to hurt her when the time came to break up.

'Come on! I've gotta get my secret Santa organised and we're going swimming with Matty and Ben in half an hour. Come on, Mum. This is going to be the best Christmas ever!'

'I thought you were almost a teenager.'

'I am.'

'Aren't they supposed to sleep until midday?'

James merely laughed and headed out to the kitchen. 'You need coffee,' he called.

No. She needed clarity because she was far too mixed up to make sense out of anything at the moment. By the time they were due to meet Matty and Ben, Tom's stomach had churned itself into a severe state of knots. Would Ben say anything more about their discussion? Should *she* say something more?

Sighing, she pasted on her debutante smile and headed out to greet them, ready for the short walk to the springs. Matty greeted her warmly with a big hug. 'Merry Christmas, Tom.'

'And to you, too.' She kissed the girl's cheek, then turned to look at her father. 'Good morning, Ben.'

'It's not good, Tom.'

'It's not?'

'Nope. It's glorious.' His smile was bright, his eyes were shining and she sighed with longing. 'Shall we go?' he asked, the two kids already running on ahead. She nodded and fell into step beside him. To her utter astonishment, Ben took her hand in his, holding it firmly. He didn't say a word, didn't care who saw them, and continued to walk and talk as though it was quite natural to stroll down the main street of the town holding her hand. She didn't know what to say or do so she did nothing, simply deciding to enjoy it. Perhaps this day was going to be as glorious as he'd promised.

'Hey, Jimmy. What are you doing?' Matty asked, looking at her friend as they walked past the vet's house.

'Shh.' He stopped and put a package on the front doorstep then ran off.

'Oh, my gosh. You're Lottie's secret Santa.' Matty's eyes were wide. 'I can't wait to get my gift. I'm so excited. I wonder who it could be.' She danced down the street, then stopped. 'I hope it's not Chit again. Last year I got Chit and although I think he's real nice, he got me a doll. A *doll!* I was eleven years old *and* I'm a tomboy, and he buys me a doll.'

'It's the thought that counts,' Ben interjected.

'I know, I know. I just hope this year's secret Santa has two brain cells to rub together.'

'Matty,' he scolded, but she merely laughed and ran ahead with Jimmy. 'Is she *my* daughter?' he asked with a laugh.

'That she is, and you should be extremely proud of her.'

'Oh, I am. I am.'

When they arrived at the springs, Tom stopped walking and simply stood looking at the breathtaking scenery around her. 'Something wrong?' Ben asked.

'No. This place…it's so incredible. It gets to me every time.' She looked around at the beautiful green trees, some smaller shrubs beneath them. The ground was covered with leaves and twigs but the path was well worn as it went between the trees and then on to the pool. A sandy bank surrounded the waterhole, along with several rocks and a few overhanging trees. The water was crystal clear and still until James climbed the tree, wiggled out onto the over-hanging branch, grabbed hold of the tyre swing, which was its main feature, and bombed his way into the water, causing it to ripple.

They had a wonderful time at the springs and, thankfully, were the first ones to arrive. They knew it wouldn't be long before they had company and so they made use of the area while they could. The instant the cool water sluiced over her. Tom sighed, loving the feel of it against her skin.

'Aah, this is definitely a little slice of heaven. So special,' she murmured as she floated, her arms stretched out wide. Ben came up beside her and slid his arm around her waist. He was tall enough to stand on the bottom and she looped her arms around his neck, feeling a little shy and self-conscious at the open intimacy.

'You're special,' he said.

Tom looked deeply into his eyes, loving the way he seemed to be caressing her soul. It was as though he was trying to show her that it wasn't just the outside that was important but *all* of her.

'Woo-hoo!' James gave a big Tarzan yell as he swung

out and splashed into the water once more. When he came up, he was quite close to them. 'Did you see that? That one was amazing.'

James swam off and Tom frowned. Had he not seen her with her arms around Ben's neck? Or was it that it simply didn't bother him anymore? Perhaps he'd meant what he'd said yesterday. That he would love to have Ben for a father.

When some more people arrived, Tom swam ashore and climbed out, gathering up her towel and sitting on one of the big rocks by the water's side. Within fifteen minutes the springs were nearly packed with early morning swimmers, enjoying the day. Christmas greetings were exchanged and everyone seemed determined to be happy and have a wonderful day. Tom laughed as she watched Ben flipping first Matty in the air and then James. After that, they had a splashing war which she was positive Ben managed to win even though the other two ganged up on him. He was an amazing father, an amazing man, and she could tell he really loved her son, just as she really loved his daughter.

Tom sighed. He was so easy to love.

Her eyes widened at the realisation. She was in love with Ben? When? When had that happened? She looked down at her hands and clenched them together to stop herself from fidgeting at this marvellous, wonderful but startling discovery. She loved Ben. There were no two ways about it. It was there and it was real.

Now there was more at stake than before. Now, if anything happened between them, it could never end. They needed to be together for ever and she wasn't sure that was going to happen. How did Ben feel about her? Should she ask him? Should she profess her love? No. If she did that, she'd be laying herself open to hurt. She'd been hurt before.

Oh, yes, Walter had hurt her badly but that had been more of a humiliating hurt. Realisation dawned that Ben had the power to hurt her much worse than Walter had. She loved him so utterly and completely, with all her heart, and she'd *never* felt that way about Walter.

'Tom?'

She looked up as Ben came to stand beside her, dripping wet but still he looked good enough to lick dry.

'Are you all right?'

What did she say? What was she supposed to say? No, I'm not all right because I've realised I'm in love with you? 'I'm fine.' She smiled at him to prove her point. 'Just thinking.'

'About what?' He laid out his towel and sat beside her.

'My secret Santa.'

'You got Matty, didn't you?'

She was stunned. 'How did you know?'

He shrugged. 'Guessed. I was watching your face when she was talking earlier and saw your smug little smile. You forget, Dr Bates, that I know you quite well.'

'You do? But you've only known me for a couple of weeks.'

'So? It can take far less than that to get to know someone—as long as they want you to know them, that is.'

'I see. Well, don't tell her.'

'I wouldn't dream of it.' They watched the youngsters playing for a while and it was then Tom realised that James had climbed onto the branch two higher than the one with the swing.

'What's he doing?' Apprehension and alarm bells began to ring.

Ben rose to his feet. 'Showing off. Trying to impress Tijana.'

Tom looked to where the girl her son had introduced her

to last night was in the water, encouraging him to jump. Matty was standing on the bank, telling him to get down and to stop being an idiot.

Tom's breath caught in her throat and when she went to call out to him, she found her voice had deserted her.

'Jimmy!' Ben called. 'Stop!' But it was too late. In horror, Tom watched her son jump off the branch to the water below. She held her breath, praying he would make it and make it safely because if he did, he was going to get one enormous lecture from her.

Then she realised he was too close to the other branches. 'He's going to hit.' Even though her lips moved, the words were thought more than spoken. She looked over to where Ben was already wading out into the water, telling the other kids to move back, to stand clear. James's foot hit the lower branch as he sailed down, knocking him off balance and sending him into the water at an awful angle. The splash was loud and for an instant the world seemed to stop revolving.

Ben dived beneath the water, swimming strongly to where James had landed. He couldn't have been under the water for more than a moment but to Tom it was an eternity. Ben hauled him up and into his arms, holding him close. When James coughed and spluttered, Tom breathed an enormous sigh of gratitude and relief. He was all right. Her son was all right. Thank goodness because now she could tear strips off him.

Ben carried him out of the water and over to her side, where she held out her arms for him. 'Come here,' she said. 'Let me look at you.'

'I'm fine, Mum,' he muttered, and she could tell he was totally embarrassed.

'That's what you think.' She gathered him into her arms, holding him close and kissing his head.

'Mum,' he moaned. 'Everyone's looking.'

'I don't care. You're my son and when you do a foolish thing like that, when you scare me half to death, I'm allowed to hold you and kiss you as though you'd just been born. Understand?' There was something in her tone that brooked no argument. 'You may be as tall as me, James Bates, but you're still my son and that gives me the right to cuddle you like this in front of everyone.'

'If it helps,' Ben said cheerfully as he sat down beside Tom, 'consider your embarrassment part of the consequences.'

'Consequences?'

'You'd better believe it, my boy. Scaring your mother like that. What were you thinking? No.' Ben held up a hand. 'Don't bother. I *know* what you were thinking and it doesn't wash. You do not impress girls with stupidity. If you do that, they only think you're stupid.'

'You're not my father,' James replied, hurt reflected in his tone.

'He may as well be,' Tom interjected, as Ben was about to speak. 'You told me yourself that you wanted Ben as a father. Well, this is what real fathers do. They care for their children, they look after them and along with the mother they form a unit to teach children right from wrong.'

'Wise behaviour from stupidity.' Ben couldn't believe the elation he was feeling at Tom's words. James wanted him as a father? He tried not to puff out his chest, tried to remain totally calm as hope soared wildly within him. He took a good look at James's foot where it had hit the water. 'You're lucky you haven't split the skin open the way your leg smacked the water.' James winced as Ben continued the examination. 'But you have sprained it. It's already starting to swell. We'd best get you back to the clinic for an X-ray.'

'But what about…' James paused, looking briefly over

where Tijana was talking with some girls and giggling a little, before meeting his mother's eyes. 'To the clinic,' he said sadly. Matty stayed while Ben carried James back into town.

'It's not broken,' Ben said, pointing to the X-ray on the screen a little later. 'You were very lucky, James.'

'It is sprained, however, which means we need to bandage it and you'll be on crutches for the next few weeks.'

'What?'

'Consider that part of the consequences, as well,' Ben replied. 'Pride always comes before a fall. Familiar with that proverb?'

James nodded, feeling rather contrite. 'Yes, sir.'

'Don't call me *sir*. I'm just Ben.'

James put his arms around the man and hugged him. Tom clutched her hands to her chest, loving the way her son loved and respected this man. This wonderful, gorgeous man whom she loved with all her heart.

Together they bandaged James's foot and found a pair of crutches for him to use. 'Go to the house and lie down.'

'Part of the consequences?'

'No. Resting your body in preparation for tonight's party. You don't want to miss that, do you?' Tom asked.

'No, ma'am. Going home right now,' he said, going out the door.

'He does pretty well on those.'

'Broke his leg when he was five. Jumped off the top of an upright piano because he thought he could fly like Peter Pan.'

'I guess once you acquire a skill you always keep it.'

'Such as?'

'Knowing the right way to impress girls.' Ben switched the X-ray machine off before coming up behind Tom and sliding his hands around her waist.

'And how's that?'

'By practising jumping from the third branch when they're not around so that when they *are* there, you do it with ease.'

Tom spun around to look at him. 'You've jumped from that branch?'

'Sure. Many times. Would it impress you if I showed you?'

'No. It would make me pass out from worry.'

'Really?' He tightened his grip, pulling her closer. 'Why is that?'

Tom looked into his eyes, seeing his need for the first time. He had doubts, he had worries, too, and she realised she had the power to solve them. Clarity. She'd finally found the clarity she'd been searching for.

'Because I'm in love with you.'

'You're…' Ben was stunned and air suddenly seemed to leave his lungs.

'I'm not telling you to burden you or anything like that. Honestly, Ben. It's just, well, I thought you should know and—'

She was cut off by his mouth on hers. For a second she couldn't move but then she sighed into the kiss, winding her arms about his neck as he pressed his body close to hers. This kiss was different from the other one they'd shared. This one was filled with promise, with respect, with hope.

'That's the best Christmas present you could have given me,' he said when they finally came up for air. 'And you're not even my secret Santa.'

'Do you know who is?'

'Lottie.'

'That's right. You watch when people pull your name out of the hat. Very clever.' What he hadn't done was say anything about her declaration, although she could possibly take the powerful way he'd just kissed her as a declaration, but it was a fuzzy one at best.

'Come on. We've got lots to do and very little time to do it in.'

'We do?'

'We do. Well, you do. Matty showed me the invitation you gave her. Having a beauty session at your house when the rains hit?'

'It was supposed to be a girl thing. Boys aren't invited.'

'I suppose you want me to keep an eye on Jimmy.'

'Yes, please. I initially thought he could help with the final preparations but now, with his leg out of action, he'll just have to sit there and watch.' She sighed. 'He was so hoping for a perfect Christmas. I really feel for him.'

'Aah, don't worry. Tijana will be impressed with his bandage and his crutches. He'll be laughing and smiling at the Christmas dinner, just you wait and see.'

'I hope you're right.' They locked up the clinic and headed next door to her house, Ben still holding her close. 'But first things first. Breakfast?'

'Sure, but what about Matty?' she asked as they walked up the steps and into her house.

'I'm here,' Matty said. She was sitting on the floor next to James, playing a game of cards. 'Thought I'd come and cheer Jimmy up.'

Tom walked by and dropped a kiss on her head. 'Very thoughtful of you.'

Ben made pancakes for breakfast and Tom couldn't believe how well he looked in her life. The four of them together—they were like a family. They all cared for each other, all needed each other, and, well, she certainly loved all three of them. She glanced at Ben again, wishing he'd give her some indication of how he felt deep inside.

Afterwards, they went to help with the final preparations for the big feast. Fitzy seemed to have ordered enough food to feed an army but she guessed that was about the size of the population at the moment, albeit a small army. She was soon beside Lin and Lottie in the kitchen, icing cakes, making punch and preparing vegetables.

'How many potatoes do we need to peel?' Lin grumbled, looking into the huge barrel Fitzy had placed before them.

'Work, women. Work!' he commanded, then left them to mutter to themselves. When she finally went back outside, Tom gasped at the transformation. Lights had been hung around the verandas of the buildings and trestle tables and chairs were stacked up neatly against the walls.

'Hey, you.' Ben sauntered over and placed a kiss on her head. He was stripped to the waist with a tool belt slung low on his hips and a hammer in his hand. Tom had a hard time trying to keep her tongue from hanging out. 'You like?' he asked, slowly turning, and she laughed, half embarrassed, half impressed.

'I do.'

'You like because you love me.' His grin was enormous and this time he pressed a smacking kiss to her lips.

'Aw, fair dinkum, Doc,' Bertie complained. He was up a ladder and was waiting impatiently. 'Leave the sheila-doc alone and get back to work. I need the hammer.'

Ben handed Bertie the hammer but returned to Tom's side.

'So, handyman Ben, I see you've let Bertie do the ladder work this time. Quite right, too. Don't need another of the men in my life hurting themselves on Christmas Day.'

Ben groaned at her teasing. 'You're never going to let me forget that, are you?' he asked rhetorically.

'Nope. Bruised coccyxes will forever remind me of you.'

Ben kissed her again. 'I love it when you talk all medical like that.'

Tom laughed and Ben explained how the town was going to be transformed. 'It's going to be great.' He spread his hand wide, pointing to the different areas. 'We'll have lights hanging across the street from building to building. We're putting the hooks in now. Once the rains finish, we'll string the lights up and then, when the sun goes down, we'll turn them on and light this place up. It'll look amazing.'

'And all the tables and chairs?'

'They'll be put out in a flash. White tablecloths. Good china, knives and forks. None of those plastic things on Christmas Day. Only the best. Christmas hats, party poppers. We've got the works. You won't believe how great this place looks when it's Christmas-dinner time.'

'And what happens if someone actually wants to drive down the road?'

'Impossible. Tonight Blaytent Springs is closed for the party. Chit's set up roadblocks and detours but I'll tell you what, if some poor soul is driving down this road on Christmas night, we're liable to make them stop and join in.'

'You're a good man,' she said with a firm nod.

'I know. And you love me.'

She laughed, trying not to show her nervousness. It was clear he didn't have any qualms in accepting her love and that was a good thing. Right? 'I've got to go,' she said. 'I need to get ready for the beauty session.'

'Is that your present to Matty?'

Tom could hear the caution in his tone. 'Don't you worry your pretty little head about it.' She patted his cheek and he caught her hand in his and brought it to his lips, kissing her wrist. It was enough to almost make her lose her train of thought. 'Where Matty's concerned, I know what I'm doing. She may be a tomboy with you but with me she's all girl. Trust me.'

'I do.' And it was there in his eyes, she could see it. She wished he'd say something but after a moment she pulled her hand back and smiled.

'I'll see you later.'

'You can count on that,' he said as she went down the steps. When she arrived at her house she expected to find Lin, Lottie and Matty there. They were the only women who lived in town and last night she'd invited them to come and pamper themselves, yet there were a lot more than three women waiting for her.

'Uh…we told a few of the girls what you were planning,' Lin said with a beaming smile, not getting up from the chair on Tom's veranda. 'They wanted to come along, too.'

Tom recognised a lot of the women she'd been speaking to over the past few days and knew there was no way she could turn them away. It was Christmas after all. She'd made up an organic recipe for a facial scrub and it looked as though she was about to make more. 'Then we'd better get started.' Tom went up the steps and turned to face them all at the door. 'Welcome to the outback beauty parlour,' she said, and opened the door.

The next hour was a mass of oestrogen and laughter. James stopped by to collect some clothes and went promptly away saying if he stayed, he'd no doubt be smothered in the gooey stuff they had on their faces. Tom watched Matty carefully and was pleased to see her joining in the fun, letting Lottie smear facial scrub onto her face.

They toned, they moisturised and then set to work on the hair. Half the time Tom felt as though she was constantly giving lessons. She took Matty aside. 'Honey, if you're uncomfortable with any of this, you just let me know. I don't want you to feel pressured into doing this.'

'Nah, it's fine.' The girl shrugged. 'It's Christmas and I've gotta admit, it's kind of fun, all being here together, tripping over each other. Hey, you know what would be really cool? We could have facial scrub fights. You know, throw it at each other and smear it all over the place.'

'Hmm. How about next year and *you* can clean it up?' Matty laughed. 'Deal.'

Would she be here next Christmas? Would she be with Ben? She sighed and looked around the room at the female bonding going on, knowing she'd never had a better time and she'd been a regular visitor at day spas for most of her adult life.

Diving back into the fray, she set about putting small curlers into Matty's short, boyish cut. 'This is gonna make me look so girly.' Matty giggled, excitement in her tone. 'It won't make me look silly, will it?' she asked quickly.

'Do you think I'd do that to you? Never, my darling. I love you too much for that.'

Matty turned to look up at her and the intensity in the child's brown eyes made Tom crouch down beside the chair. 'I love you, too, Tom.' Matty put her arms around Tom's neck and the two embraced. 'So does my dad,' she whispered in Tom's ear.

'Does he? He hasn't said anything.' As they parted, Tom found it impossible to hide her fears.

Matty simply shrugged. 'He's a guy.'

'True,' Tom agreed, as though that explained everything, and got back to work, fixing Matty's hair. As the giggling and fun continued, Matty became more and more relaxed so that when Tom stood her in front of the mirror, a touch of blusher, a dash of mascara and a light lip gloss applied to her lips, her blond hair bouncing slightly around her face, Matty simply stared.

'That's not me.' But her lips moved in time with the words. 'It *is* me. Wow! I look…I look…'

'Stunning. And about seventeen. Oh, no. Your father's not going to like that.'

Matty was still busy staring at her reflection. 'I look… like a *girl.*'

Tom laughed. 'You ain't see nothin' yet, sweetheart.' Taking her hand, she took the girl into her bedroom and went to the cupboard, taking out two boxes. 'This one,' she said, holding out the smaller of the two, 'is from your secret Santa.'

'Oh, my goodness. Is that *you?*'

'It is. I'm sorry it's not so secret.'

'I don't care.' Matty ripped open the Christmas paper and squealed at the shoes there. They had a small wedge heel with straps that came up her legs.

'Specifically chosen so they don't throw your spine out of alignment, don't hurt your legs or your feet.'

'I hope I can walk in them.' That was all she said as she pulled them out of the box and began putting them on. Tom helped her and when they were done, Matty admired them.

'And now for this.' Tom held out the larger box. 'Merry Christmas, Matilda.'

As though she'd guessed what it was, Matty opened the box and pulled out a gorgeous sundress made out of the softest fabric she'd ever felt in her life. 'It's… Oh, Tom. It's…the absolute coolest *ever!*' She held the garment up against her and sniffed.

'Just as well I applied waterproof mascara.' Tom helped her change and then the two of them embraced.

'I never thought I'd enjoy feeling like a girl.'

'You probably weren't ready before today.'

'Dad's gonna freak. Big time.'

'Do you think he will?'

'Sure. Now he has to think up a different punishment for me if I drink alcohol before I'm eighteen.' They looked at each other and laughed, knowing she spoke the truth.

As the rain slowly started to ease, the women got ready to leave, ready to rush back to their own homes to get changed for the party.

'Tom.' Lin embraced her. 'Thank you. We've all had the most marvellous time.'

'It was very generous of you to provide everything,' Lottie agreed.

'It was my pleasure.'

'It was fantastic,' Lin said. 'Being out here, surrounded by blokes, I sometimes forget that I'm a woman, that we're allowed to dress up and wear make-up and be girly.'

'So had I,' Lottie agreed. She touched her hand to Tom's cheek. 'You and your son have been a real breath of fresh air for this town, a real blessing.'

Lin stabbed a finger at Tom. 'Don't you even think of leaving.'

Tom merely smiled. 'Go and get dressed. We're gonna knock those guys' socks off.' As they left, Tom turned to find Matty lying back in the chair, her feet up on the coffee-table as she read a book. 'You can dress her up…' she began, and laughed.

'Now that you've transformed everyone else in the town, it's time to do you,' Matty said, waving her away to her room. 'Go. Thank goodness you can transform yourself in a tenth of the time it takes the rest of us.'

A little later, Tom came out and presented herself to Matty. Their dresses were of a similar style, the skirts swirling around at midthigh, the bodices fitting them to perfection, but where Matty's had centimetre-wide straps, Tom's was strapless.

'Ooh. The final touch. I almost forgot.' Tom went to a box and pulled out her flashing Christmas tree earrings, putting them on. Then she handed Matty a pair. 'Clip-ons,' she said. 'But they flash just the same.'

Matty laughed as she put them in place and turned them on. 'Dad is totally gonna freak now!'

Tom slung her arm around the girl she was desperate to call *daughter.* 'You know something, Matty, I think he is. Let's go gauge his reaction.' As they left the house, she picked up two other parcels. One large one, one long thin one.

'What's in there?'

'Presents for James and your dad.'

'What did you get Dad?'

Tom only smiled. 'You'll see.' They headed over to Ben's house, where she knew he and James would be waiting for them—Matty walking perfectly in the new shoes and not falling over once.

James came to the door on his crutches and when he opened it, although he had seen his own mother dressed up in this way many times, he gaped, mouth wide-open.

'You'll be catching flies in a moment,' his mother said.

'Hey! Who's letting the flies in?' Ben demanded, coming to the door to see why Jimmy was standing there with it wide-open. 'Jimmy. Shut the—' He didn't get any further as he came to stand by the boy he desperately wanted to call *son.* 'Whoa!' He stared at Tom, his warm gaze caressing her all the way down and all the way up. 'Lady, you are amaz-ing.'

'Thank you.' Tom inclined her head towards Matty and Ben reluctantly tore his hungry eyes away to look at the young woman beside her. Tom couldn't help the laugh as he recognised who it was.

'*Matty!*'

'I know,' James said softly.

'Matty! I didn't recognise you. I thought you were one of the visitors from out of town.' He took her hands in his and stepped back for another look. 'Sweetheart, you're... Wow! You're beautiful, Matty. Not that I've never thought you weren't beautiful, honey. You've always been beautiful to me. Always,' he quickly clarified.

'I know what you meant, Dad. I'm still amazed at the transformation myself.'

'We'd better go in. The flies. Remember?' Tom said, and the two stunned males moved back. James hobbled over to the lounge. 'You look nice, darling.'

'Thank you.'

'Here.' She handed him the larger parcel. 'Merry Christmas.' James was as eager to tear off the paper as Matty had been and when he opened the box, he burst out laughing.

'What is it?' Matty came closer to get a better look and James pulled a hat out of the box.

'It's a Christmas cork hat.' He looked at the outback hat with strings dangling down but where there were usually corks, designed to keep the flies away from the face, this hat had little plastic Santas dangling down instead. James put it on his head and grinned. 'It's perfect.' James blew her a kiss.

'I'm glad you like it.' Then Tom turned to Ben. 'Here.' She shifted from foot to foot, feeling a little self-conscious. 'Merry Christmas.'

Ben seemed surprised but took the box she held out to him. Carefully, he removed the paper and she smiled to herself, surprised. For some reason she'd thought he would have been a ripper, not a careful remover and folder, but that was exactly what he was doing now, folding the paper and putting it on the table.

'Oh, will you get on with it, Dad?' Matty's impatience was starting to overwhelm her.

Ben opened the box just a crack and peered inside. The smile on his face was slow but ended up being as broad as they came.

'What is it?' James asked, similarly impatient.

'A tie.'

'A *tie*. Dad doesn't wear ties.'

'Trust me. He'll wear this one.' Tom watched as he took it from the box.

'He will, indeed,' Ben replied. 'If you'll teach me how to tie it.'

'You don't know?' There was just so much she didn't know about this man yet she loved him so completely. The little things…the little things were important and she was looking forward to finding out what they all were, if he'd give her the chance. 'Here.' She took the tie and spun him around so his back was to the children. Once she'd tied it, she pressed a little button that was sewn inside the tie at the point.

Ben laughed then turned to face his audience. The tie was a Christmas one, with a picture of a large Christmas tree, the tie getting wider at the bottom as the branches got bigger. The tree was also decorated, with lights—flashing lights.

'Hey. Not fair,' James said. 'My hat doesn't flash.'

Tom fixed him with a look. 'That's what you think. Look closer at the band.' And sure enough, within a moment James's hat had little lights flashing around the band of the hat.

'Well, don't we all look like a walking advertisement

for Christmas?' Ben remarked. Then he crooked his arm to Tom. 'Shall we go?'

'We shall.' Tom nodded, feeling way beyond happy.

Hours later, with most of the food eaten and the noise level increasing, Dezza went inside and put on the Australian Christmas carols, everyone joining in and dancing in the street. The secret Santas had revealed themselves but much to Tom's disappointment, no one had approached her. She hadn't received a gift and she kept telling herself not to get upset about it. It was just so hard when she'd entered into the spirit of the game, really enjoying herself. It is better to give than to receive, was one proverb that kept going around in her mind, and she forced herself to smile, not wanting anything to mar this wonderful night. With people singing and dancing and generally making merry, Ben whispered something in Tom's ear and took her hand, leading her away from the noise and kerfuffle.

'I've been waiting for the perfect moment to get you alone,' he said.

'Oh? Why is that?'

'Well, partly so I can nuzzle you.' He gathered her close into his arms as they stood on the back veranda of the hotel, secluded and out of sight of everyone else.

'Mmm, I like it when you nuzzle.'

'Of course you do, because you love me.'

'You keep saying that.'

'I just need to keep reminding myself of the best Christmas I've ever had—and I'm not talking about the tie.'

'Why do you need to keep reminding yourself?'

'Because I've been rejected in the past.' His tone was completely serious. 'Just like you, Tom, I've been hurt in affairs of the heart, and while my circumstances are very different to yours, betrayal is still betrayal. Being told by legal messenger that your wife has begun divorce proceedings when she doesn't even talk to you about it first, when she doesn't even make any attempt to discuss issues, to attempt to reconcile, when that happens, Tom, it makes a man very vulnerable. Then, years later, a woman comes into his life—a woman so amazingly different from anyone he's ever met—and within less than an hour of meeting she tells him that 'nowhere' is more a state of mind than anything else—well, how can you possibly blame that man for falling in love with her and being totally floored that she loves him back?'

'You... You love me?'

Ben smiled but it disappeared as his eyes became intense. 'How could you doubt that?'

'You didn't say anything.'

'I thought my actions spoke louder than words. I told you yesterday that once I started touching you, I knew I wasn't going to be able to stop, and today I've held your hand, I've kissed you, I've had you as close to me as I dared, given everything that was going on. When you told me how you felt this morning, well, I...I still can't believe it.'

'You had better because I don't love or trust easily, or so I thought. Coming out here, though, I've realised it's easy to trust when people are genuine.'

'What you see is what you get.' He nodded.

'I hope so.' Her smile was sexy and was definitely inviting him to come hither.

'Just a moment,' he said, reaching into his shorts pocket and pulling out a box. 'Happy secret Santa,' he said.

Tom gasped. 'You! You're my secret Santa! I was wondering what had happened. I thought I'd missed out.'

'Never.'

'I can't believe you drew my name out of the hat. How amazing is that?'

'Actually, not that amazing. I had to swap with six different people before I found out who had you.'

'Oh, Ben.' Tom laughed and shook her head. 'The lengths you'll go to.'

'It was worth it. Open it.'

She did, being as careful with the paper as he'd been, and when she saw the piece of plastic mistletoe in the box she couldn't help but laugh. 'It's perfect.'

Ben withdrew it and held it over their heads. 'I made a pact not to kiss you under the mistletoe. Well, right here, under the mistletoe, I intend to revoke that pact and make one that says I can kiss you any time I want for the rest of my life.'

'Now, that pact I like.' Tom looked up at the mistletoe. 'But do you think we really need it?'

'Probably not,' he said, and tossed the plastic plant aside, preferring to hold her with two arms than one. Unable to keep his mouth away from hers any longer, Ben lowered his head. When they came together for their first kiss since mutually declaring their love, Tom sighed, unable to believe the extent of her feelings for this wonderful man.

'I love you,' she whispered against his mouth. 'We've got to make this work, Ben. We've just got to.'

'We will.'

'There's so much at stake. Matty. James.'

'Not to mention me helping you to accept the fact that you weren't to blame for your husband's infidelities.' Ben shook his head. 'It wasn't you, my darling. It was him. He was weak. He was greedy. How anyone could *ever* think of cheating on you is beyond me. He didn't deserve you, but I do. I deserve you so very much and I want you to know that I cherish you, I adore you so completely, my Thomasena.'

This time he pulled a much smaller box from his other pocket and held it out to her. This one wasn't wrapped in paper and slowly he opened it and went down on one knee, holding out the diamond ring.

'Tom—I love you. You're an amazing woman, an amazing mother, and I know for a fact you'll be an amazing wife. Marry me?'

'Ben.' She looked at him with all the love in her heart, knowing exactly what her answer would be, but first she decided to tease him a little—after all, it was the outback way of doing things. 'Well…there is one condition,' she said, and saw his jaw clench slightly in anticipation. 'Will you teach me how to whistle the way you do? I've always wanted to learn.'

Ben relaxed and laughed, nodding enthusiastically. 'Absolutely. We'll make an outback sheila out of you yet, my darling city princess.'

With that, Tom took his face in her hands and urged him to his feet. 'Oh, Ben!' She kissed him, tears of utter happiness and joy sliding down her cheeks. 'Yes. Oh, yes! Of course I'll marry you.'

He took her trembling left hand in his and slipped the ring on. 'Perfect fit.'

'It's beautiful but if you don't mind me asking—how did you get a ring out here?'

'What? You don't think I didn't have a diamond engagement ring just lying around the house, waiting for some incredible doctor to smash into my life and knock me for a six?'

'No. I don't.'

'Well, you're wrong. The ring belonged to my mother. My parents enjoyed forty-nine years of marriage before my father passed away. My mother died two years ago and I inherited her ring, hoping that one day I'd meet the woman worthy enough to wear it.'

'Ben. It's beautiful. If I had every ring in the world to choose from, *this* is the one I'd choose.' She held it out and they admired it, sparkling in the artificial lights strung around the hotel.

'We'll make it work, Tom.'

'Of course we will.' She swallowed. 'How do you think the kids will react?'

Ben shrugged. 'Positively, I hope.'

'Shall we go and find out?'

Ben slipped his arms about her and drew her to his heart. 'In a minute.'

'More than one, I hope.'

'Dr Bates! Really!'

EPILOGUE

'YOU promised me last year we could have a facial gunk fight,' Matty said, looking firmly at her stepmother. The past twelve months had been one of utter happiness and love. They'd added on a few rooms to Ben's house and after the wedding, which had taken place in March, they'd started their life as a family.

Tom and James loved their new life in the outback and with Ben and Matty in their lives, it was as though they'd finally found their place in the world—a place where they were all blissfully happy. Ben had even helped Tom to begin reconciling with her parents, something she'd thought would never happen.

'I also remember saying you'd be the one to clean it up,' Tom warned, lifting a handful of the facial mixture in retaliation.

'Ladies,' Lottie said, trying to calm them down as the two circled each other in a totally unladylike fashion, grinning wildly. They made a good team, Matty and Tom. Tom had been able to guide Matty through the rocky waters of becoming a woman, while Matty had taught her stepmother how to let loose and have fun, to be a tomboy every once in a while.

With a war cry Matty let her handful fly but Tom was too quick for her and ducked, the 'gunk', as Matty called it, landing on Ben, who'd just that instant walked in the door. 'Oops,' his daughter said, trying to smother a laugh.

'Matilda!' Ben wiped the facial mixture from his face and peered at his daughter. He advanced slowly, his expression letting her know he wasn't at all amused. Tom was watching him closely, though, and as he neared the bowl, his fingers scooped up some of the mixture and then, in a lightning-quick move, he plastered it into his daughter's hair. Matty squealed with surprise.

'What's going on?' James asked, running in the door at the scream from his stepsister. Tom straightened.

'Just a bit of father-daughter bonding,' she said, but was then hit with some of the mixture herself. She wiped it away and looked at her husband, noting the extremely guilty look on his face. 'Thank you, darling.'

'You're most welcome, honey.'

James stood by her side, laughing until his mother rubbed her hands together and slathered the mixture onto his face. James was stunned for a moment and all four looked at each other. They were at different sides of the room, the bowl of mixture in the middle.

At the same moment they all rushed towards the bowl, grabbing handfuls and hurling them at each other.

'You're mad. All quite mad,' Lottie said, and Lin agreed, the two women deciding to stand outside on the veranda for a while.

'Yes, we are,' Tom yelled back, laughing. 'We're one big, mad, happy family.'

'Never a truer word was spoken, my wife,' Ben said, taking her in his arms and dipping her backwards in a romantic gesture. He pressed his mouth to hers, amazed at how the love he felt for her simply kept increasing every day—and he knew, without a doubt, it was the same for her. He didn't even mind when she slathered the mixture into his hair. After all, having fun within a marriage was perfect.

BRIDES OF PENHALLY BAY

Medical™ is proud to welcome you to Penhally Bay Surgery where you can meet the team led by caring and commanding Dr Nick Tremayne. For the next twelve months we will bring you an emotional, tempting romance – devoted doctors, single fathers, a sheikh surgeon, royalty, blushing brides and miracle babies will warm your heart...

Let us whisk you away to this Cornish coastal town – to a place where hearts are made whole.

Turn the page for a sneak preview from
Christmas Eve Baby
by Caroline Anderson
– the first book in the
BRIDES OF PENHALLY BAY series.

CHRSTMAS EVE BABY
by
Caroline Anderson

Ben crossed the room, standing by the window, looking out. It was a pleasant room, and from the window he could see across the boatyard to the lifeboat station and beyond it the sea.

He didn't notice, though, not really. Didn't take it in, couldn't have described the colour of the walls or the furniture, because there was only one thing he'd really seen, only one thing he'd been aware of since Lucy had got out of her car.

Lucy met his eyes, but only with a huge effort, and he could see the emotions racing through their wary, soft brown depths. God only knows what his own expression was, but he held her gaze for a long moment before she coloured and looked away.

'Um – can I make you some tea?' she offered, and he gave a short, disbelieving cough of laughter.

'Don't you think there's something we should talk about first?' he suggested, and she hesitated, her hand on the kettle, catching her lip between those neat, even teeth and nibbling it unconsciously.

'I intend to,' she began, and he laughed and propped his hips on the edge of the desk, his hands each side gripping the thick, solid wood as if his life depended on it.

'When, exactly? Assuming, as I am, perhaps a little rashly, that unless that's a beachball you've got up your jumper it has something to do with me?'

She put the kettle down with a little thump and turned towards him, her eyes flashing fire. 'Rashly? *Rashly?* Is that what you think of me? That I'd sleep with you and then go and fall into bed with another man?'

He shrugged, ignoring the crazy, irrational flicker of hope that it was, indeed, his child. 'I don't know. I would hope not, but I don't know anything about your private life. Not any more,' he added with a tinge of regret.

'Well, you should know enough about me to know that isn't the way I do things.'

'So how do you do things, Lucy?' he asked, trying to stop the anger from creeping into his voice. 'Like your father? You don't like it, so you just pretend it hasn't happened?'

'And what was I supposed to do?' she asked, her eyes flashing sparks again. 'We weren't seeing each other. We'd agreed.'

'But this, surely, changes things? Or should have. Unless you just weren't going to tell me? It must have made it simpler for you.'

She turned away again, but not before he saw her eyes fill, and guilt gnawed at him. 'Simpler?'

she said. 'That's not how I'd describe it.'

'So why not tell me, then?' he said, his voice softening. 'Why, in all these months, didn't you tell me that I'm going to be a father?'

'I was going to,' she said, her voice little more than a whisper. 'But after everything – I didn't know how to. It's just all so difficult – '

'But it *is* mine.'

She nodded, her hair falling over her face and obscuring it from him. 'Yes. Yes, it's yours.'

His heart soared, and for a ridiculous moment he felt like punching the air, but then he pulled himself together. Plenty of time for that later, once he'd got all the facts. Down to the nitty-gritty, he thought, and asked the question that came to the top of the heap.

'Does your father know it's mine…?'

She shook her head, and he winced.

'Have you had lunch?' she said suddenly.

'*Lunch?*' he said, his tone disbelieving. 'No. I got held up in Resus. There wasn't time.'

'Fancy coming back to my house and having something to eat? Only I'm starving, and I'm trying to eat properly, and biscuits and cakes and rubbish like that just won't cut the mustard.'

'Sounds good,' he said, not in the least bit hungry but desperate to be away from there and somewhere private while he assimilated this stunning bit of news.

She opened the door, grabbed her coat out of the staff room as they passed it and led him down the stairs.

They walked to her flat, along Harbour Road and up Bridge Street, the road that ran alongside the river and up out of the old town towards St Piran, the road he'd come in on. It was over a gift shop, in a steep little terrace typical of Cornish coastal towns and villages, and he wondered how she'd manage when she'd had the baby.

Not here, was the answer, especially when she led him through a door into a narrow little hallway and up the precipitous stairs to her flat. 'Make yourself at home, I'll find some food,' she said, a little breathless after her climb, and left him in the small living room. If he got close to the window he could see the sea, but apart from that it had no real charm. It was homely, though, and comfortable, and he wandered round it, picking up things and putting them down, measuring her life.

A book on pregnancy, a mother-and-baby magazine, a book of names, lying in a neat pile on the end of an old leather trunk in front of the sofa. More books in a bookcase, a cosy fleece blanket draped over the arm of the sofa, some flowers in a vase lending a little cheer.

He could see her through the kitchen door, pottering about and making sandwiches, and he went and propped himself in the doorway and watched her.

'I'd offer to help, but the room's too small for three of us,' he murmured, and she gave him a slightly nervous smile.

Why nervous? he wondered, and then realised that of course she was nervous. She had no idea what his attitude would be, whether he'd be pleased or angry, if he'd want to be involved in his child's life – any of it.

When he'd worked it out himself, he'd tell her. The only thing he did know, absolutely with total certainty, was that if, as she had said, this baby was his, he was going to be a part of its life for ever.

And that was non-negotiable.

* * * *

Brides of Penhally Bay
*Bachelor doctors become husbands and fathers –
in a place where hearts are made whole.*

Snuggle up this festive season with
Christmas Eve Baby
*by Caroline Anderson
– out in December 2007!*

FREE

4 BOOKS AND A SURPRISE GIFT!

We would like to take this opportunity to thank you for reading this
Mills & Boon® book by offering you the chance to take FOUR more
specially selected titles from the Medical™ series absolutely FREE!
We're also making this offer to introduce you to the benefits of the
Mills & Boon® Reader Service™—

> ★ **FREE home delivery**
> ★ **FREE gifts and competitions**
> ★ **FREE monthly Newsletter**
> ★ **Books available before they're in the shops**
> ★ **Exclusive Reader Service offers**

Accepting these FREE books and gift places you under no obligation
to buy; you may cancel at any time, even after receiving your free
shipment. Simply complete your details below and return the entire
page to the address below. You don't even need a stamp!

YES! Please send me 4 free Medical books and a surprise gift. I
understand that unless you hear from me, I will receive 6
superb new titles every month for just £2.89 each, postage and packing
free. I am under no obligation to purchase any books and may cancel
my subscription at any time. The free books and gift will be mine to
keep in any case.

M7ZEE

Ms/Mrs/Miss/Mr...Initials ....
BLOCK CAPITALS PLEASE

Surname ....

Address ....

....

....Postcode ....

Send this whole page to:
The Reader Service, FREEPOST CN81, Croydon, CR9 3WZ